About the Book

Life in the latter days of the nineteenth century was as exciting to a "nine-going-on-ten-year-old girl" as it is to the more sophisticated young miss today.

True, Georgie Clark and her friend, Susan Hamilton, did not possess the latest walking and talking dolls, but they found as great a pleasure in making clothes for their rag dolls as today's ten-year-old girl does in purchasing a complete, ready-made wardrobe for her doll.

There was no television in the 1889's and 1890's to amuse and entertain young people, but there was a fascinating new invention—the "talking machine"—that made its appearance during Georgie's childhood.

Devoted parents and a happy home life were part of Georgie's fun-filled days. So were the snowball fights with the Smith boys, the annual Fourth of July celebration, the church entertainments, her friendship with the daughter of the Sioux Indian chief, the sleigh rides behind the Clark's faithful horse, and, especially, Georgie's first ride on the mule-drawn streetcar.

But Georgie had a purpose in life—to help Pierre become the state capital. Although the story of Georgie is fictional, it is based on the historical fact that Pierre became the capital of the new state of South Dakota in 1890. How Georgie contributed to this event is the essence of the story of *Georgie's Capital*.

GEORGIE'S CAPITAL

GEORGIE'S CAPITAL

by Martha Sutherland Coon

Illustrated by Corinne Keyser

HARVEY HOUSE, Inc.
Publishers
Irvington-on-Hudson, N.Y. 10533

To Carolyn, Ann, Janice,
Cindy, Debbie Ann,
Susan, Julie and Barbie

Library of Congress Catalog Card Number: 67-16905
Manufactured in the United States of America

HARVEY HOUSE, INC. • *Publishers*
Irvington-on-Hudson • New York

Contents

Chapter 1
Georgie's Friends

In the pioneer town of Pierre, South Dakota, on December 12, 1889, Georgianna Clark (Georgie for short) and Susan Hamilton plowed through loose, fluffy snowdrifts on their way home from school at noon recess.

The Smith twins, Richard and Charles, walked close behind the girls, trying to kick snow into the tops of their overshoes.

"We know something about Georgie's papa that you don't know!" Charles yelled.

"I know everything about my papa!" Georgie screamed.

"I bet you don't know this," Richard bragged, "because it happened just last night."

"At our house when you were asleep," Charles added.

"Probably you were asleep, too, and dreamed it," Susan teased, as she turned suddenly and threw a handful of snow at Richard. Then she ran, slipping and sliding, as Richard aimed a big snowball at her.

"Wait for me, Susan!" Georgie called. Then she turned to Charles. "What do you know about my papa?" she asked.

"He was elected chairman of the Pierre-for-Capital Committee," Charles replied, walking up even with Georgie.

"Oh, that!" Georgie exclaimed, "that's over! Even first graders know that Pierre is already the capital of South Dakota. The election was in October."

"But it's true," Charles insisted. "We got out of bed to listen."

"You were probably so sleepy that you got it all wrong," Georgie told him.

They were still arguing about it when they caught up with Richard and Susan at Center Street, where the boys had to turn up the hill to go home.

"Didn't they say that, Richard?" Charles called, "that Mr. Clark was to be the new chairman?"

"Of course," Richard said. "You ask your papa when you get home, Georgie."

"I dare you to tell your papa that you got out of bed and listened," Georgie yelled.

The boys replied with a storm of snowballs as they turned off Capitol Avenue.

"Now we're all messed up!" Georgie complained. She took hold of Susan's hand and ran until they reached her side gate near the end of the block.

"I'll ask my papa right now," she told Susan. "I'm sure he'll say the boys are wrong." Then she stood, patting the black nose of the horse that stood at the hitching post, and watching Susan turn the corner and go up Huron Street past the front gate.

When Susan was out of sight, Georgie opened the side gate and stamped along the brick walk and up the seven steps to the side porch, trying to shake the snow from her overshoes and coat as she went.

Britta came out of the kitchen with a broom. "Stand still until I brush off snow," she said.

Britta was the hired girl from "the old country." Her face was sunburned, and her straw-colored hair was pulled back into a bun so tightly that it seemed to draw her straw-colored eyebrows up onto her red forehead. She had strong arms, and she brushed hard.

"Look out!" Georgie complained, "you'll tip me over!"

"Take off your overshoes," Britta added, "I just scrubbed the floor."

She made it sound like, "Ay yoost scrubt da floor." Georgie always wanted to laugh at the funny way Britta talked, but Mama said that would be unkind to a girl who really spoke English very well for having been in America only a year. So Georgie turned her face away from Britta and opened the door, after she took off her overshoes.

In the warm kitchen, Britta put Georgie's blue coat and hood and red leggings and mittens on a chair by the cookstove. "Wash hands here." She pointed to the wooden sink.

Georgie pumped cistern water into the tin basin in the sink and scrubbed her hands with the stinging yellow soap that Britta made from lye and bacon drippings. She whirled the roller towel to a clean place and dried her hands. Then she opened the sitting-room door and tiptoed through.

"Now I'll ask Papa," she thought.

The round table in the middle of the room was set for lunch. Papa and Mama were facing each other across the white linen tablecloth. Linnie, Georgie's three-year-old sister, sat in her highchair between them.

"Hello, Dodo!" Linnie called.

Papa was saying earnestly, "There isn't anything in the world that I want more—not even to be elected myself."

When he saw Georgie, he stopped and began again in a different voice, "Why are you so late, Georgie?"

Georgie loved Papa so much that she couldn't bear to be scolded by him. Instead of answering, she stood still and looked at the floor.

"Didn't you hear Papa?" Mama asked.

"I'm sorry," Georgie replied, sliding into her chair.

"That doesn't tell me why," Papa insisted.

Georgie tucked her napkin into the neck of her blue flannel dress as she said, "Susan and I had an argument with the Smith twins, and we got into a snow fight."

She was going to tell Papa what the argument was about, and to ask if the twins were not wrong, but Papa said, smiling, "That's my Georgie—always in action!" which meant that he wasn't going to scold. Then he turned to Mama and began to talk about some coal that was to be delivered that afternoon.

Georgie had been taught never to interrupt grown people, so she stuffed mashed potato and creamed beef into her mouth, thinking that she would ask her question when Papa was through talking.

But he had so much to say about that coal, such as, "Be sure to have him throw water on the load so that the dust doesn't come through the floor, and to bank up the window when the coal is in," that he was still giving directions as he put on his coat. Even as he went through the door into the kitchen, he continued. "I'm sorry to load such a dirty job on you, Lucy, but I can't get away from the office this afternoon." So there was no chance at all for Georgie to ask him anything.

As she hurried with her lunch, she wondered whether Mama could answer her question. But Mama had followed Papa into the kitchen and was still out there, talking to Britta.

Georgie wondered what it was that Papa wanted even more than he wanted to be elected attorney general. She wished she could get it for him, whatever it was. She decided that she would ask about it when she asked about the mistake that the Smith boys had made.

Linnie jumped down from her chair and ran to the bay window that looked out toward the side

gate, so that she could watch Papa untie Harry and drive away to his office.

Georgie swallowed the last of her potato as she folded her napkin and put it into its silver ring. Then she followed Linnie and helped her to pull aside the heavy lace curtain so that they could stand behind it.

Papa had stopped on the side porch to put on his overshoes, and now they saw him running down the brick walk and through the gate to the post where Harry was stamping and snorting. The wind lifted Papa's derby off his brown hair. He grabbed it back and jammed it down hard on his forehead.

While Harry tossed his black mane and pawed with his black feet so that snow flew over the dashboard into the sleigh, Papa pulled the strap out of the iron ring on the post and tied it into a ring on Harry's harness. Even through the double storm window, Georgie could hear the sleigh bells jingle as Papa worked. Then he stepped into the open sleigh, tucked the buffalo robe over his knees, and unwound the reins from around the whip.

The girls blew kisses to him when he looked up at the window. He put a kiss on his gloved hand and made a big fuss about blowing it back to them. When he had blown two kisses, he slapped the reins over Harry's back, making him jump and start to run.

Then Linnie went to find Mama, but Georgie stood behind the curtain, watching what was going on in the sitting room.

Britta had already cleared the table and was putting on the red and green damask cloth it wore between meals.

Mama came back from the kitchen and sat down in her low sewing rocker, pulling Linnie into her lap.

Linnie was such a baby! She wouldn't take a nap without being rocked. Georgie couldn't remember having been so little. Now she was nine and in the fourth grade. She was even big enough to take care of Linnie sometimes.

Mama's lullaby suddenly had funny words. She sang, "Georgie, you must not hang on the lace curtains, or you will tear them. Come out of the window right away and start back to school."

The words did not fit very well into the tune of "Rockaby, Baby," so Georgie came out giggling from behind the curtain. She opened her mouth to tell Mama the joke on the Smith twins, but Mama put her finger on her lips and shook her head, as she pointed to the kitchen, so Georgie quietly went out and put on the wraps that Britta had dried.

That joke about the twins and the capital would have to wait until after school.

Chapter 2
The Capital Fight

When Georgie came home at four o'clock, she noticed that heavy clouds were darkening the sky, so it seemed especially bright and cosy to find Mama darning stockings, with her feet on the fender of the baseburner. A lighted lamp stood on the walnut stand beside her. In the warm nook behind the stove Linnie was singing to her rag doll.

Georgie stood in the front hall for a moment after she had hung up her wraps, looking at Mama's pink cheeks and at the lovely coils of red-brown hair on top of her head. Georgie liked to look at pretty people. She wished she were not so mousy-brown and dumpy.

Mama called, "Come and keep me company, Georgie. How was school today?"

Georgie pulled her willow rocker up even with Mama's and sat down, putting her feet beside Mama's on the fender.

"The twins are awfully stupid, Mama," she began. "They think there is still a Capital Committee and that Papa is its chairman. Isn't that a joke on them?"

Mama exclaimed, "You children! You're as interested in politics as grown people. It's amazing!"

"Why?" Georgie asked. "Why wouldn't we be interested? Papa talks all the time about politics. He talked all last year about getting the capital, and so did Mr. Smith and Mr. Hamilton. And now we've got it, and Papa talks all the time about running for attorney general. Why wouldn't I be interested?"

"Well," Mama replied, "some children wouldn't get so excited about it. What is this about the twins?"

"They told Susan and me that they listened at their bedroom door last night and heard Papa being elected Chairman of the Pierre-for-Capital Committee. And Pierre has been the capital for eight whole weeks. How can they be so wrong?"

"Darling, that election in October was just for one year—for the temporary capital. Next November the people must choose a permanent capital."

Georgie asked, very much surprised, "You mean we'll have to do it all over again?"

"Yes, we do," Mama said soberly, "and it's true there was a meeting at Mr. Smith's last night and Papa was chosen . . ."

Georgie hardly ever interrupted, but she couldn't wait to find out. "And if we win, we'll have to keep doing it over and over?"

"No, indeed!" Mama answered. "If we win this time, Pierre will keep the capital always. And Papa says he wants Pierre to win this election more than he wants anything in the world."

"So that was what he was talking about at lunch!" Georgie put in.

"Yes, indeed!" Mama answered, "and of course it is especially important to him because, if he is elected and Pierre loses, Huron will be the capital, and we'll have to move to Huron."

Georgie squeezed her eyes shut so that she could think about this news. She had never been to Huron, but she was sure she would not like living there. Besides, if they had to move away from Pierre, she couldn't play with Susan.

"I want to stay in Pierre," she announced anxiously, opening her eyes, "and I want Pierre to be the capital for always. It's got to be the capital! And I want to help! Please, Mama, can't I help some way?"

"You are an eager little bunny," Mama said smiling. "The best help you can give is to be a good girl. You'll help very much that way."

Georgie looked earnestly into Mama's eyes before she replied. "Naturally, I always try to be as good as I can, but I want to help in some important way. Isn't there some job I can do?"

Mama reached over her sewing basket and patted Georgie's cheek. "Maybe Papa can find something for you to do. I'm sure he'll be pleased that you want to help. Now, why don't you play with Linnie while I see what Britta is cooking for dinner."

Georgie jumped out of her chair. "Come, Linnie," she said, "let's play 'Boo.' "

While Linnie put her doll away, Georgie thought, "I'll ask Papa tonight how I can help him."

That evening when Papa came into the house, bringing cold, fresh air from outside, Georgie shouted, "Oh, Papa!" meaning to ask her question right away. But Papa swung Linnie to the ceiling before he kissed her; he rumpled Georgie's hair, saying, "How's my girl?" and he looked at Britta, who was setting the table for supper. Then he said, "Dinner must be almost ready," and hurried through the parlor into the front bedroom, without giving Georgie any chance to ask her question.

Georgie knew that Papa would come out all scrubbed and brushed for dinner, so she said to Linnie, "We'd better wash our hands, too." She took Linnie into their bedroom and carefully poured water from the big, pink-flowered pitcher into the pink-and-white washbowl.

"When you are nine," she began, as she washed Linnie's hands, "you can pour water all by your own self, the way I do." As they both dried their hands on the big towel, Georgie added, "Let's not play any more. We can watch Britta until dinner is ready." So they sat together in Papa's big red wooden rocker and watched Britta put dinner on the table.

Georgie had decided long ago that dinners were more important than breakfasts and lunches because Britta always dressed up for dinners. Tonight she wore a freshly ironed blue calico dress with white buttons down the front of its tight bodice, and a big white linen apron with heavy lace across the bottom.

As the two girls rocked, they saw Mama come in from the kitchen, her cheeks very pink from standing over the hot stove. She pulled off her big calico apron as she hurried to the front bedroom.

When Britta rang the little silver bell that always sat in the center of the table and took her place behind Papa's chair, Georgie said, "We'd better go to the table." She helped Linnie climb onto her chair and tied her bib. She was pleased that Papa and Mama came to the table almost immediately, because she knew Britta's feelings would be hurt if the dinner got cold before it was served.

Papa pulled out Mama's chair and seated her very formally before he sat down in his big chair and bowed his head. Then they all bowed their heads while Papa said, "For what we are about to receive, O Lord, make us truly thankful." Georgie liked it that Britta bowed her head, too.

Then Papa sliced the roast and filled the plates with meat, potatoes, and gravy. Britta took each plate and set it between the dish of peas and the little round butter plate that marked each place. Then she passed a plate full of slices of her freshly baked bread before she went back to the kitchen.

Georgie ate very carefully, because she felt responsible for setting Linnie a good example of table manners. When Mama had promoted her to sit beside

Linnie at dinner and to help her, she had said, "Table manners are very important for a lady. We want Linnie to be a lady when she grows up, just as you will be. And little Linnie will copy everything her big sister does. So be very careful."

So Georgie did not fill her spoon or fork too full; did not scrape her plate; did not complain about the food even if she didn't like it; and did not speak unless she was spoken to.

The grownup talk was not very interesting tonight, so Georgie had plenty of time to think about helping Papa.

When they were all through with their meat and vegetables, Mama rang the silver bell for Britta to clear the table and to bring the dishes of baked rice pudding to each one.

Linnie was already nodding over her dinner, so Mama took her off to bed, leaving Papa and Georgie at the table. Georgie felt very grownup to be eating alone with Papa.

When she put away her napkin, she said, "Mama told me about the new capital fight. Do you think maybe we will have to move to Huron?"

Papa looked up quickly. "Not if I can help it! We beat Huron last October, and I think we can do it again if everyone works hard enough. Why do you ask? Don't you think you are pretty small to be worrying about capital fights?"

Georgie pushed the hair out of her eyes. "I want to help, because I don't want to move to Huron. Then I wouldn't see Susan any more. Besides, I want us to win."

Papa's eyes twinkled under his heavy brows. He said, "Right you are! Pierre for the capital!"

Georgie could never tell for sure whether Papa was laughing at her inside his mind. She didn't like being laughed at.

"I want to help the Capital Committee," she said, trying to sound grownup. "I could lick stamps."

"Stamps?" Papa asked, pulling his eyebrows together, as if he were puzzled. "Oh! Stamps! You want to be one of my secretaries? Well, if I run short of help, I'll call on you."

"I want very much to help," Georgie repeated, going close to him and laying her hand on his sleeve.

Papa patted her hand. "The very best way for you to help is to be Papa's good little girl."

"Oh!" Georgie replied in a small voice. It was no use trying to explain. She stood still, letting Papa pat her hand.

"Mama is looking for you, pet. Kiss me good-night and run to bed."

Georgie obediently kissed Papa and walked slowly to the bedroom door where Mama was standing. She was determined not to cry, for that would make everyone think she was too little to help.

She went through with her usual program of undressing and kneeling by the bed to say her prayers. But after Mama had tucked her in and had gone back to Papa in the parlor, she slid out of bed and knelt down again.

In a very tiny voice that she hoped God would hear, and that Mama wouldn't, she prayed, "Dear God, I want to help Papa get the permanent capital for Pierre. Please find a way for me to help. Amen."

Then she climbed back into bed, pulled the blankets over herself and Linnie, and cuddled down close to her little sister. She felt sure that God would show her something to do to help Papa.

Chapter 3
Saturday Fun

As Georgie took her play dress from the hook on Saturday morning, she worried a little because God had not put any new ideas into her head while she was asleep. "But I'm sure He will, pretty soon," she thought. "Maybe if I help Mama, I'll think of some way to help Papa."

So, as soon as she had finished her bowl of oatmeal and cream, she asked Mama, "What do you want me to do today?"

"Why don't you entertain Linnie by stringing buttons?" Mama suggested. She took a big box of buttons from her sewing basket and put it on the floor near the baseburner. "This is a nice warm spot for you to sit," she said. "I'm going to be busy working with Britta. I'll expect you to keep Linnie out of my way."

"Come, Linnie," Georgie called, "you open the box while I thread the needles."

As they made necklaces of the sparkly buttons, Georgie felt importantly grownup to be threading Linnie's needles and helping her to poke their points into the tiny holes, but she couldn't see that it had anything to do with getting the capital. She wished that she could think of a real good way to help Papa.

When Mama called that it was lunchtime, Georgie said, "Let's race to see who can pick up the most buttons." They raced so fast that when Mama came into the room, all the loose buttons were in the box.

"My, my!" Mama said, as she put the box away, "what good little housekeepers I have!" She smiled especially at Georgie. "You are a very good helper. Now please see that Linnie is washed up for lunch."

"It doesn't seem like time for lunch," Georgie answered, as she dried Linnie's hands.

"Papa isn't coming home this noon, so we're having lunch early," Mama explained.

Georgie was disappointed. She had thought maybe Mama would tell Papa what a good helper she was at home, and Papa would realize that she was old enough to be a helper in his office.

Since luncheon without Papa was a short meal, and since Linnie took her nap right afterward, Georgie soon found herself with nothing to do. She decided to go out to her "own house" and plan about helping Papa get the capital.

Georgie's "own house" was a space under the side porch. It was enclosed with green-painted lattice strips nailed in a diamond pattern. Where the porch backed up against an angle of the house, there was a tiny door. It was blocked now with snow, but Georgie pulled until the door was open wide enough for her to creep through. Then she stood up straight under the porch.

The "house" had a soft, fluffy, dust floor. Today some snow had sifted through the lattice and had made a lacy pattern around the edge of the floor. The back wall of the "house" was the red brick foundation of the real house. The furniture was chunks of firewood for stools and orange crates for tables. Linnie could not get in unless Georgie helped her, and no grown person could creep through the tiny door, so Georgie felt as if it was very much her own house. It was a good place to go when she wanted to think.

While she thought, she mixed dust with snow to make a mud cake for Linnie, which she frosted with pink icing made with dust scraped from the bricks in the wall.

Papa had talked at dinner as if the secretaries in his office would lick the stamps, so that idea was no good. Georgie wished she were big enough to be a real secretary. She wondered whether she could help by picking paper scraps off the office floor and by emptying the wastebaskets. Surely the committee would need help in keeping the office neat. "I'll ask Papa about that tonight," she decided.

When the mud cake was ready, Georgie set it in the middle of an orange-crate table. "It really looks very nice," she said to herself, as she carefully squeezed through the tiny door, pushed it shut, and piled snow up against it so that no dog or cat could sneak in and spoil the cake. Then she went into the house to find Linnie.

Linnie pulled at Georgie's hand and begged, "Play horsey, Dodo!" When she was too small to say "Georgie," she had said "Dodo," and sometimes she still liked to talk baby talk.

"Guess what Dodo did," Georgie said. "She made a frosted cake for Linnie. It's in the little house under the side porch."

"I want to go see it," Linnie cried, tugging at Georgie's hand.

"When Mama lets you go outdoors," Georgie said. "Let's play horsey now. Shall Dodo put Linnie on the big horsey?"

The big horse was Papa's rocker which had broad, flat wooden arms that were easy to sit on.

Linnie climbed onto one of the arms, faced the ladder back of the chair, and held on with both fat little hands.

Georgie sat on the other arm and rocked the chair, until it began to slide across the ingrain carpet. When they had rocked across the room and had banged into the dining table, Georgie dismounted, carefully turned the chair around, and then rocked it back to its usual position by the bay window.

Linnie screamed every little while that she was falling off. "That's because we ride sidesaddle," Georgie explained, "but ladies must always ride sidesaddle."

They were still having fun riding the chair when Mama came in from the kitchen. "My goodness!" she exclaimed, when she saw what they were doing.

Georgie slid off the chair arm. "I did it to amuse Linnie," she said, "you said we could—sometimes."

"It wears out the carpet," Mama said, "but maybe that's better than Linnie's fussing. Anyway, it's time for Saturday baths. Who will be ready first?"

Linnie jumped down beside Georgie. "I be!" she cried, "I be first!" Then she ran into the bedroom.

Georgie hurried after her. When they were both stripped down to their undies, they danced into the kitchen in their long-sleeved, long-legged union suits with buttoned-up flaps in the back.

Mama and Britta had brought the round wooden washtubs from the back shed and had set them by the kitchen stove. Now they were filling them with warm water from the tank at the end of the stove.

Mama caught Linnie, pulled off her undies, pinned her long, red-gold braids tight to the top of her head, and plopped her into one tub.

Georgie pulled off her own undies, but she let Britta pin up her stubby, brown braids. Then she jumped into her tub with such a splash that Mama looked up from soaping Linnie and frowned a cute little frown. "Britta just scrubbed the floor," she said, "be careful not to splash." Then she gave Georgie an oval cake of sweet-smelling soap. "This is better for a lady's complexion than that lye soap in the sink."

Georgie sniffed at it. "I like this kind," she said, "it smells sweet, like lilacs."

When Britta picked up a washcloth, Georgie said quickly, "I can do myself," so Britta gave her the cloth and sat down by the tub. Once in a while she pointed to an elbow or a knee and said, "More!" so Georgie knew Britta really wanted to do the scrubbing. That made Georgie try hard to get every corner clean, so that Britta would not interfere.

After Britta had helped to dry her, as she stood close to the warm stove, Georgie wriggled her way into her clean woolen union suit, which felt a little scratchy in comparison with the one she had been wearing. Britta then buttoned her pantywaist down the back and helped Georgie to draw on a pair of ruffled muslin panties and button them to the waist. After that came two ruffled muslin petticoats.

Then Britta folded the legs of the union suit neatly around Georgie's ankles and drew up the long, black woolen stockings over the folds to fasten the stockings onto the elastic straps that hung down from the pantywaist. "Here's your dress," she said.

When the freshly washed and ironed navy blue woolen dress had been buttoned, Georgie sat down to put on her own shoes. While she tugged the buttons into their buttonholes with her own pink-handled buttonhook, she thought with pleasure that tomorrow was Sunday, and that she could wear her new shoes. Mr.

Olsen, the shoemaker, had made these for her by hand. The soft, fine kid uppers, blacked very shiny, fitted perfectly, and the soles, made of layers of good leather pegged together, squeaked in a delightful way when Georgie walked. She could hardly wait for a chance to squeak down the aisle in church.

When Linnie was dressed, the two ran into the parlor, where Papa was waiting for them. Tonight he sat between them on the sofa and told them stories about his boyhood in the wild forests of Wisconsin.

"I was so afraid of bears," he began, "that one time when I was sent on an errand about dusk, and saw a big stump by the road on the way home, I thought it was a bear. I ran screaming all the way home. Then your grandfather said, 'Don't be a coward, George,' and he lighted a lantern for me and told me to walk back along the road and look for that bear. I was afraid the bear would get me if I did that, and I was afraid your grandfather would spank me if I didn't."

"Did you?" asked Georgie, wondering if she would have dared to do the same thing.

"Yes, I did," Papa replied, "and I saw that it was just a stump. It taught me to be brave."

Then they heard Britta ringing the little bell for dinner, so Papa stood up and took hold of their hands.

"Perhaps I'll tell you another story next Saturday night," he promised, as they walked to the table.

After dinner Papa took down the beautiful polished wooden blocks that he had given Georgie on her sixth birthday and began to build some castles with many windows and towers. But Linnie couldn't wait for a castle to be finished. After she had spoiled two fine castles, Papa remarked, "Castles are too grownup for Linnie."

Georgie suggested, "Let's build towers for her to crash." That was more fun for everybody.

Mama came to watch Linnie crash a tall tower. "Tomorrow is Sunday," she warned them. "You must go to bed soon, or you'll oversleep and make us late for church."

Papa added, "But we haven't practiced the Sunday-School verses."

"Hurry then—where are the cards?" Mama asked. She helped Papa and Linnie put away the blocks, while Georgie got the little picture cards that had Bible verses on them.

"I put them here to be safe," she explained as she reached under the big family Bible on the stand between the windows.

"These two are yours, Linnie," she said, "and don't bend them because when you get ten, and can say all the verses to your teacher, she'll take these little cards and give you a big one to keep."

Linnie gave her cards to Mama. "I can say them," she said. Then she stood very straight, her hands at her sides, and recited, "Praise the Lord," and "Be kind."

"That's right," Mama said. "Now, Georgie!"

Georgie's verses were longer, and she had to say some of them twice to get them right. Then she put all the cards back under the Bible.

Papa threw Linnie up into the air and caught her in his arms. She also rode on his shoulder, giggling, until Papa dumped her onto her bed.

Mama put her arm over Georgie's shoulder as they walked to the bedroom. Then Mama undressed Linnie, and Papa helped Georgie with her buttons. As he worked with them, Georgie asked, "Papa, couldn't I empty wastebaskets at the Capital-Committee office?"

"They are too big for you," Papa answered, "and besides, we have a young man hired to do that kind of work. But maybe we can find some way for you to help, later. Don't worry so much about it."

But as Georgie felt herself drifting off to sleep, she thought how very much she wanted to help Papa get the capital for Pierre.

Chapter 4
Sunday

When Georgie opened her eyes the next morning, she saw that Mama, who was coming into the room, had her hair curled on wads of paper pinned all over her head. Georgie knew that Mama had curled her hair that way so that she might look especially nice for Sunday. It was a very special day, and you must look your best when you went to church.

Linnie punched Georgie in the side. "Sunday dresses!" she cried. "I like Sunday dresses." She pointed at the sky-blue jumper that Mama was taking out of the closet. After Mama had hung it over a chair, she brought out Georgie's dark-green cashmere jumper, and then laid a white china-silk guimpe on top of each dress.

Georgie leaned over the bed and looked for her new shoes. Sure enough, they were waiting for her. She jumped out of bed onto the cold carpet and wiggled into her union suit as fast as she could. When that was on, she was comfortably warm and could take her time about the rest of her clothes. When she reached for her guimpe, Mama said, "Put your red wrapper on until after breakfast. Come here, Linnie, and let me button your wrapper, too."

After they had finished their breakfast of pancakes and maple syrup and all the cups of milk that they wanted, they scrubbed their teeth with the toothbrushes that were kept in the pink-flowered holder on the washstand.

Then Mama put Linnie on her toilet chair, but Britta gave Georgie her coat and led her through the back shed and out the back door. "You're big girl, now," she said.

"I'm almost grownup, now, Britta," Georgie replied. Then she ran along the frosty white sidewalk to the privy at the far end of the yard. It seemed a long time since she was so little that she could not go out there alone.

When she came back, she very carefully latched the back door, because Mama had said, "Only very little girls would forget to latch doors when they come in." Then she ran to the bedroom, washed her hands in the basin on the washstand, and put on her church dress.

Mama had to help Georgie to fasten the middle buttons down her back. "You are growing up so fast, Georgie," she said. "Now you are able to button all but two of them."

Georgie thought, "If I am so nearly grownup in two things, why does Papa think I'm not big enough to help the Capital Committee?"

"Now go into the sitting room and be still until Papa and I are ready," Mama said.

Linnie sat in the big rocker, and Georgie sat in Mama's low chair until Papa came out of the front bedroom. Then Georgie went close to him to touch the smooth cloth of his Sunday suit. "I just love that shiny feel," she said. He was pulling at a coattail of his Prince Albert coat to reach its secret pocket, and Georgie could smell the perfume on the white linen handkerchief that he was tucking away. "Lilac!" she said, sniffing, "I love that best of any."

"Mama will put some on you, if you ask her." Papa smiled at her over his tall collar and big black cravat.

"Fumery!" Linnie screamed, running into the front bedroom.

As Georgie pulled at the edge of Papa's coat to make it hang evenly just a little below his knees, Mama called, "George, is your shirt front all right? Britta said she had trouble with the starch."

"Very nice," Papa answered, running his fingers over the smooth tucks. He pushed the shirt front farther down inside his low-cut vest. Georgie knew he did that because most of the shirt was of plain muslin that was not supposed to show. Only the tucked front was of fine linen.

"You look very nice, Papa," she said, before she started to follow Linnie into the front bedroom.

"Oh, Mama! You have on your new plum-colored dress!" Georgie cried, when she saw Mama standing in front of the mirror. "It looks lovely! Mrs. Larson is a real good dressmaker, isn't she?"

"I think she did pretty well on this," Mama replied, holding up her hand mirror so she could see her back in the big mirror. "Have I got the bustle in the middle?"

Georgie looked carefully at the tight bodice, the skirt draped over a full bustle in the back, and the pleated ruffles at the bottom. "It's all right," she said. "You look real pretty."

Mama dabbed some cologne water on Georgie's forehead before she slipped into her long overjacket lined with pale blue silk. She tied her plum-colored satin bonnet with its blue lining and caught up her gloves and handkerchief. Georgie, watching, admired the way the blue ostrich tips waved and danced on top of the bonnet as Mama dashed through the door.

Then Georgie hurried to the front hall for her own coat and hood. She brought them into the sitting room to warm in front of the stove while she put on her overshoes.

"You'd better move a little faster," Papa called, as he draped Mama's long black satin cape with its fur collar over Mama's shoulders. Then he set his shiny stovepipe hat on his head and picked up his gloves and gold-headed cane, before he followed Mama to the front door where Linnie was calling, "Please open the door!"

By the time Georgie had clamped all the buckles on her overshoes, tied her hood, and buttoned her coat, the family was out of sight. She dashed through the door, across the frosty porch, and jumped down the steps, landing on her back on a strip of ice. She hopped up, brushed off her coat as well as she could, and skated along the sidewalk to catch up with Papa.

"Georgie!" Mama cried, "have you forgotten that this is the Sabbath Day?"

Georgie slowed down and walked to the corner where Papa was waiting for her. "Why is it wicked to run on Sunday?" she asked, as she slid her mittened hand into his gloved hand.

" 'Remember the sabbath day to keep it holy,' " he quoted. "Also the Bible says we should do all things decently and in order. We shouldn't make ourselves late so that we think we have to run."

The cold air felt good on Georgie's hot face; it even tasted good when she opened her mouth to take a breath. The hard, tramped-down snow crunched under her feet. The drifts alongside the walk reflected shining pricks of light. When Georgie squinted through her eyelashes, as she held tight to Papa so that she would not fall, she saw tiny rainbows. "I love walking to church!" she exclaimed.

The church bell had been saying a gay "Ding, dong," but now it changed to a slow "Dong, dong."

"It's tolling!" Mama said. "That means it is almost time for service to start."

"I'll carry Linnie," Papa offered, "so that we can walk faster."

As they stepped through the church door, Georgie was relieved to see that the sexton was still pulling on the bell rope, so they had time to take off their overshoes and leave them in the entry.

Georgie's shoes squeaked very nicely as the family walked down the aisle to the front row of chairs. Papa motioned for Georgie to go into the row first, to the chair right beside the organ.

Georgie had never been so close to the organ before. She saw now that it had pedals almost as big as the treadle on Mama's sewing machine. The organist had to pull up her tightly draped skirt in order to pedal. She pulled it so high that Georgie could see her black silk stockings above the tops of her shoes. Georgie felt ashamed to look at the lady's legs, but she could not tear her eyes away from the disgraceful sight until the choir began to sing. Then she looked at the two ladies and the two gentlemen who were the choir.

The ladies wore draped merino wool dresses like Mama's. One was black, and one was brown. The blonde lady had bangs that hung down from the front of her bonnet. The brunette lady had little spit curls in front of her ears. Both ladies held their song books very far out in front of them, as if they wanted to show off their gloves.

The gentlemen wore Prince Albert broadcloth coats like Papa's. They held their books far out also, but with only one hand, hiding the other in the back pocket of the coat. One man had a fluffy moustache like Papa's, and the other had a heavy black beard that covered his chin.

After church the Sunday-School superintendent arranged the big chairs into two circles and brought the red kindergarten chairs from where they had been stacked against the wall. He made a circle of the red chairs for the "Infant Class." Linnie went over there and sat down beside her teacher, Miss May.

Susan Hamilton's mother taught the middle class that Georgie belonged to.

Papa taught the Bible Class for the older people. His class talked so loud that Mrs. Hamilton had to make her class lean their heads into the middle of their circle so that they could hear one another.

"It would be nice to have a classroom of our own," Mrs. Hamilton told the class, "and maybe we will some day, if Pierre keeps the capital, and if business improves so that we can afford to make the church larger."

"Getting the capital is the most important thing in the world, isn't it?" Georgie asked.

"Well, no," Mrs. Hamilton replied, "loving God and reading the Bible and going to church are much more important." But she patted Georgie's shoulder as she spoke, so Georgie knew that Mrs. Hamilton understood how she felt.

Then Mrs. Hamilton went on with the Bible lesson. Before she dismissed the class, she asked if anyone had memorized ten little verse cards.

"I know eight," Georgie said, taking a card from the box in Mrs. Hamilton's hand, "and this makes nine."

"I'll have a big card ready for you in two weeks," Mrs. Hamilton said, smiling.

After Sunday School was dismissed, people talked about the capital. Georgie listened as they asked Papa how they could help.

Papa told them all, "Report to headquarters, and we'll keep you busy."

Georgie wondered how one reported, and where headquarters was. She did want to be kept busy helping to get the capital, but she didn't interrupt Papa as he talked. She couldn't ask on the way home, either, for Papa gave Mama his arm and motioned for the girls to walk behind them. Georgie decided she'd have to wait until after dinner to find out.

When they reached home, they changed their Sunday dresses for everyday clothes and sat down to one of Britta's especially good Sunday dinners.

When Georgie had finished the last crumb of her apple pie, she remarked, "That was a good dinner—what are we going to do now?"

Papa answered, "I'm going to take a nap." He sat down in his big rocker with his feet up on a stool and the *Advance* magazine over his face.

Mama said, "When I get Linnie down for her nap, I'll play the Bible game with you."

"I'll get out the cards, then," Georgie offered. "I like that game."

When Mama read a statement from a card, such as, "A shepherd boy who wrote songs," Georgie quickly answered, "David!" and got the card. They took turns reading, and when Linnie waked up, Georgie had almost as many cards as Mama.

"That's a good way to learn about the Bible," Mama said. "If you study the Bible carefully, perhaps you will teach a class in Sunday School when you grow up."

"I would like to teach the Infant Class," Georgie decided, as she put the cards away.

Then Papa woke up. "Who wants to ride?" he asked.

"We do!" the girls shouted together, so Papa put on his coat and went to get Harry.

Mama was helping Linnie into her coat when Georgie, who was watching in the bay window, shouted, "There he is!" Then Georgie hurried into her wraps, and they all ran out to the hitching post where Harry was pawing and snorting.

Papa tucked all of them into the sleigh, with Linnie in Mama's lap and Georgie in between him and Mama. Then they were off, the wind in their faces, sleigh bells jingling, and Harry's feet sounding clop-clop on the hard snow.

Papa said, "Well, let's look over the Capital City."

"You say that every time we go for a ride," Georgie told him.

"I never get tired of looking at our beautiful town," Papa answered, waving his whip at the statehouse. "There is the best site in the state. Nothing so handsome outside the Black Hills." He pulled Harry to a stop.

"Can you see how it would look with a great stone building set back in a planting of trees, and a fountain playing over a flower garden in front?"

Georgie squinted her eyes at the plain gray frame office building, standing a few feet back from the sidewalk, and tried to imagine what Papa was describing.

"There could be a lake where Hilger's Gulch is," Mama remarked.

"Ah!" Papa said, "that's the way it will be some day—if Pierre keeps the capital."

"It would be the most beautiful capital in America," Georgie added, softly.

"Let's take a look at the bridge," Papa suggested, turning Harry toward the river. "That's one of the best talking points we have, because this is the only bridge across the Missouri River in the whole state."

When they reached the riverbank, Georgie saw that the bridge was a sort of sidewalk or runway, with a fence on each side. It rested on little boats that barely showed above the river ice and the drifted snow.

As they were looking, a man drove up with a team hitched to a heavy wagon.

"Going across, Herb?" Papa asked.

"Yes, sir, Mr. Clark. This bridge is a great thing. I used to drive across on ice in the winter, and ferry over on the *Jim Leighton* in summer. Once I lost my team in an airhole—swept away under the ice. Now I can drive over to Fort Pierre as safe as up the road to the statehouse. It's a great thing for Pierre!"

He swung his long rawhide whip over his horses, and they clattered onto the bridge. Georgie watched them, wishing Papa would drive onto the bridge.

"Can't we go over, too?" she begged.

Papa looked at his watch. "Too late now," he said. "We must be getting home. Some day I'll take you over."

He clucked at Harry and slapped him with the reins as they turned away from the river.

Georgie said, "Any people who don't want Pierre to be the capital must be very stupid, or else they haven't seen Pierre."

"Most of them haven't seen Pierre," Papa replied. "We're planning a campaign to bring lots of visitors to Pierre this year to show them what a live town we have."

He clucked some more until Harry began to run. They slid along, sleigh bells tinkling, until Papa pulled up in front of their house and jumped out.

Mama handed Linnie to Papa, who made her stand beside him until he had helped Mama out of the sleigh.

Georgie felt very in-between. She was too big to be lifted like Linnie and too little to be helped like Mama, so she stood on the edge of the sleigh and jumped, missing the sidewalk and landing in a pile of snow.

"That child!" Mama exclaimed. "She'll kill herself yet."

"She's all right," Papa said. "Let her do it her way!"

In the house, when Papa had finally come back from putting up Harry and was hanging his coat in the hall, Georgie had a chance to ask him privately about headquarters.

"Why, that's my office," Papa replied. "You've been there."

"It wasn't headquarters when I was there," Georgie said. "I want to report to headquarters, and be kept busy working for Pierre for the capital, the way you told people after Sunday School."

"Oh!" Papa said. "I'll have to take you down there sometime. You might like to hear me make a campaign speech into a wonderful machine we have there. Now you run into the kitchen and help Mama to get supper. You know that Britta has Sunday evenings off."

"Yes, Papa," Georgie replied, feeling sure that she could hardly wait for the time to go to headquarters.

As she set the table and, after their bread-and-milk supper, helped Mama clear it again, as she helped to dry the dishes and put them away, and even after she was undressed and in bed, Georgie thought about headquarters. She thought she would like very much to hear Papa make a campaign speech. If campaign speeches were very important, maybe she could make one. She wondered whether girls were allowed to make speeches. Finally, she went to sleep, thinking that she would very much like to help Papa by making a good campaign speech.

Chapter 5
The Fourth Grade

On Monday morning Georgie waited at the front gate for Susan, who came slipping and sliding down the hill, waving her arms, and calling, "I've got a new riddle!"

"Like the old sculptor Phidias that made statues perfectly hideous?" Georgie asked.

"No, this is really a new one. Who is the greatest traveler on earth?" She danced alongside Georgie saying, "You can't ever guess."

Georgie guessed "Marco Polo," but that wasn't right. Then she guessed "Magellan," but that wasn't right, either.

At the next corner, the Smith twins turned onto Capitol Avenue. They guessed "Columbus" and "Sir Francis Drake."

"No, no!" Susan shouted. "You'll never guess it."

"Don't tell us," Charles said, "let us try some more."

At Yankton Street, Erma and Amy Brown joined the crowd. They guessed "Cortez" and "Sir Walter Raleigh."

"I'll have to tell you," Susan said. "It's a washerwoman, because she spreads her sheets, crosses the Line, and goes from Pole to Pole."

"That's good," Richard said. "I'm going to learn it and tell my papa."

But Erma asked, "What's the Line?"

"The Equator," Georgie answered.

"And the North and South Poles," Charles added.

"And sails are called sheets," Susan explained. "Oh, my goodness!" she added, "there's the last bell."

They all stopped talking and began to run as fast as ever they could. Charles and Richard beat, but the girls were close behind them. They were all out of breath when they raced past the janitor, who was pulling the bell rope beside the door. No matter what the clock in the classroom said, it wasn't "late" until the bell stopped. The janitor winked at Georgie as she ran past him.

Once he had told her, "I don't like to see little folks kept in after school for being tardy, so I always ring until I'm sure they have time to get to their seats."

Today he rang the bell so long that Georgie even had time to get a drink of water from the tin dipper in the pail on the cloakroom bench.

The riddle about the traveler had made Georgie think about geography. While the third grade recited reading up front, Georgie thumbed through her geography book, looking at pictures of Columbus and other great explorers. Then she remembered that geographies told about capitals, too, so she looked at the list of state capitals to see if Pierre were printed there. But she couldn't even find South Dakota. She was so interested in trying to find something printed about Pierre that she forgot that this was the period to study arithmetic.

When Miss May called the fourth grade forward for arithmetic, Georgie pushed her hair back from her eyes and went slowly to the front seat she shared with Susan. Georgie wasn't ready for arithmetic.

Miss May spoke. "Georgie, you may go to the board and explain the first problem."

Georgie wanted to say that she hadn't solved that one, but her voice wouldn't come out of her throat, so she silently took her book to the board and copied the first problem. Then she stood there, feeling terribly hot and uncomfortable. The longer she stood, the hotter she felt. There were tears under her eyelids, but she told herself she would not cry—she just would not cry in front of the whole class!

"Can't you do it?" Miss May asked, in a very surprised voice.

Georgie still couldn't speak, so she shook her head; then she put the chalk on the ledge below the blackboard and walked back to her seat. She felt sure that they were all thinking how stupid she was.

"What's the matter?" Susan whispered, as Georgie sat down.

Georgie just shook her head. She didn't want to talk to anyone, not even to Susan, so she shook her head at Susan again and looked very straight at the board where Erma was explaining the problem.

At the end of the lesson, Miss May said, "You may go to your seats, all except Georgie. Georgie, please come here to the desk."

Georgie's heart began to beat fast. She had seen Miss May slap naughty pupils with her ruler. Was

Miss May going to slap her? She walked very slowly to the desk.

"Georgie, you were looking at a book all last period, but it wasn't arithmetic, was it?" Miss May began.

"No, ma'am," Georgie replied.

"And you knew you ought to be studying arithmetic, didn't you?"

"Yes, ma'am."

"What were you reading? A storybook?"

"No, ma'am."

"Well, what, then?"

Probably Miss May would think she was a queer girl, but Georgie didn't know what to do except to tell the truth. Getting ready to be laughed at, she answered, "I wanted to see Pierre and South Dakota printed in the geography, but I couldn't find them. I forgot about arithmetic."

But Miss May didn't laugh. "Why, of course, I expect that would puzzle you," she said. "I can explain why if you will bring your geography here."

Georgie went to her desk for the book, sure that everyone in the room was looking at her. It seemed a long way to the desk, and when she reached it, she fumbled the books on it so that they all slid to the floor. She picked them up and piled them on the slanting surface, only to realize that she had put the geography at the bottom of the pile. Before she got everything straightened out, some of the children had begun to giggle at her. She hurried back to Miss May's desk, feeling hotter than ever.

Miss May opened the book to the first page. She said, "Look! This line of print tells when the book was published. The date is 1886. Now South Dakota wasn't a state until this past fall, 1889, so the people who wrote this book couldn't tell about it, or about Pierre being the capital."

Miss May turned the pages, saying, "After a while we shall study about territories. Here it says, 'Dakota Territory—capital, Yankton.' That's the way it was in 1886. When we get new books, South Dakota will be in the list of states, and Pierre will be listed as its capital—that is, if we win the election next November."

She smiled at Georgie. "Now that you have geography off your mind, do you think you can get your arithmetic?"

"Yes, ma'am," Georgie assured her, "but I watched all the work at the board so I can do the problems from memory, now."

Miss May brought out a different book from her desk. "Here are ten problems of the same kind. Do these on the board and then study your spelling."

"Yes, ma'am, thank you," Georgie said and went to the board. Before she even began to write the first problem, she looked through her eyelashes at the other children. She was glad to see that they were not paying any attention to her, but were studying or whispering or passing notes, as usual.

By working hard, she soon finished all the sums. After the third grade was through with spelling, Miss May came to look at the board.

"You got these eight right," she said, erasing them. Then she showed Georgie what was wrong with the other two. "Now go to your desk and study," she added, when she had erased the last problems.

Georgie went back to her seat, quite happy about her arithmetic, but worried about Pierre. If Pierre didn't win in November, it wouldn't be printed in the new geographies. The books would say, "Huron, capital of South Dakota," and she would probably be in some school in Huron, where she didn't know anybody. She just had to do something to help Pierre keep the capital.

After she went home from school, she kept on thinking about the capital. Even while she was playing with Linnie, and while Papa and Mama were talking at dinner, she thought about it.

After dinner, Mama said, "Georgie, you must be worn out! You haven't said two words since you came from school. I think you'd better go to bed right away."

"Yes, ma'am," Georgie answered. She didn't mind being sent to bed, because it was easier to think in the quiet bedroom than in the parlor where Papa and Mama were talking.

Georgie undressed quickly and knelt by the side of the bed to say her "Now I lay me . . ." prayer. Then she climbed into bed and let Mama tuck the quilt around her and kiss her good-night.

When Mama had gone and had shut the door, Georgie thought about helping by making some sort of campaign speech. She thought a long time about what kind of speech a little girl could make, and where she could find an audience who would listen to her.

When the idea finally came, she almost jumped out of bed for joy. It seemed so simple—why hadn't she thought of it sooner?

She remembered that she had asked God to help her. "I ought to thank Him for helping me think of this," she told herself. So she slipped out of bed and knelt down. "Thank you, God," she whispered.

Then she crept back beside Linnie and planned what she would say in her speech. She thought so hard about it that she thought herself to sleep.

Chapter 6
Christmas Eve

"Come here and put on your new dress, Georgie," Mama called on Christmas Eve. It was the night of the Sunday-School program, and Georgie and Linnie were to speak pieces. Georgie was happy to have a new dress to wear. As Mama buttoned it, Georgie ran her fingers over the smooth, hard-twisted poplin.

"It even feels pretty," she said, admiring herself in the mirror. "May I have some perfumery, too?" she asked, tracing the red-and-black-plaid pattern with her finger.

Mama put dabs of cologne water behind Georgie's ear and in the middle of Linnie's forehead.

"I wish my hair would be in curls like Linnie's," Georgie complained.

"Your hair looks very nice with that red ribbon on your ponytail," Mama said. "Straight hair is pretty when it is well brushed."

Even in the excitement of getting ready, Georgie kept thinking that this was to be the night that she would make her campaign speech. But she hadn't told anyone about it. It was to be a surprise.

Papa said, "The snow that fell yesterday hasn't been cleared off the sidewalks yet, so Mama and I will drag you girls on your sleds."

"I can walk just that one block," Georgie objected.

"You don't want to be all mussed up and damp when you speak your piece," Mama said. "You'd better ride on your sled."

So Georgie sat down on her sled, thinking that Mama was right. In fact, it was even more important than Mama realized, for Georgie to make a good impression tonight.

As she breathed the cold, fresh air and looked at the sky full of twinkling stars, she practiced her speech over and over in her mind. "I must wait just a little minute after I say my Christmas piece, before I begin my Pierre speech," she told herself, "and I must say it very plainly. If it sounds like a very good speech, Papa maybe will have me say it again to help the campaign."

Georgie imagined everyone crowding around afterwards to congratulate her. Papa and Mama would stand, one on each side of her, and hold her hands, and be very proud of her.

In the middle of her thinking, she heard Susan's voice shouting, "Merry Christmas, Georgie!" The Hamiltons were coming up just behind them, and Susan was on a sled, too.

Georgie called back, "Merry Christmas, Susan!"

They were almost at the church now. In the light of the gas lamp at the corner, Georgie saw many dark figures moving toward the church door. "There's going to be a big crowd to hear my speech," she thought happily.

Inside the church entry, Susan and Georgie unbuttoned their coats and looked at each other's new dresses.

"I love your red and black," Susan began.

"Your green cashmere is very becoming," Georgie said politely, although she liked her own dress much better. Before she could tell Susan to listen for a surprise at the end of the program, Mama pulled at Georgie's hand.

"Come," she said, "it's filling up, and we don't want to stand."

When Papa opened the inside door, Georgie gasped, "Oh, how beautiful!"

The big brass lamps that hung on chains were burning very dimly and were pulled up close to the ceiling, so that the room was almost dark.

On the low platform, up front, a big cedar tree shone with lots and lots of lighted candles in tin holders. These winked and blinked at the blue cedar berries, the white strings of popcorn, and the little red net stockings full of candy strung over the tree.

Linnie danced a step ahead of Mama. "Oh! Oh!" she screamed. Mama pulled her back. "Hush, Linnie," she chided. "This is the church—be quiet!"

Papa found two chairs near the front and waved Mama and Linnie to one. Then he sat down on the other and took Georgie on his knee.

Georgie looked around for Susan. Susan was looking for her, too, and waved from her seat alongside her papa and mama in the front row.

The tree dazzled Georgie's eyes so much that she could not see very well, but after a while, she noticed the Smith twins sitting between their father and mother, and the Brown family just behind them. Erma and Amy saw her and waved to her.

She was glad that so many of her best friends would hear her speech.

The superintendent stood in front, as he said, "We turned the lamps low so that you could enjoy the candlelight, but now if some of you tall young men near the door will give us some lamplight, we shall sing 'O Little Town of Bethlehem.' "

Two young men pulled the lamps down on their brass chains and turned up the wicks; then they pushed the lamps high enough so that they could walk under them.

The organist pulled out the stops so that the sound would come out strong. Although Georgie nearly wiggled off Papa's knee, she couldn't see how high the organist's skirts were this time.

Georgie liked to sing with Papa, trying to hold onto the melody against his strong baritone voice. She sang as loud as she could all the way through "O Little Town," "It Came Upon the Midnight Clear," and "Silent Night."

After the songs, Miss May read a Bible story and introduced her Infant Class. Each one of the children recited a poem or said a Bible verse.

When Linnie stood up beside the tree, she looked so pretty that Georgie felt very proud of her, with her golden hair floating out in a cloud around her. But she forgot her verse! She put her finger in her mouth and thought a while. It should have been, "Peace on earth!" Mama tried to whisper it to her, but Linnie seemed too confused to hear. Finally she took her finger out of her mouth and cried, "Hosanna! Hosanna! Hosanna!" Then she ran to Mama.

The people clapped more for her than they had for anyone. Georgie was very much pleased that Linnie was so quick-witted. Another little girl had gone back to her seat without saying anything.

After all the Infant-Class members had said their pieces, Mrs. Hamilton introduced the Intermediate Class. Georgie's hands grew damp and sticky as one after another of her classmates said their pieces. Finally she heard her name, and it sounded as if it had been spoken a very long way off.

Papa gave her a little push to make her slide off his knee. She was glad that she was the last speaker, so that she would have a good chance to make her campaign speech afterwards, but her heart was beating so fast that it almost choked her.

When she turned to face the people, she felt a little scared that there were so many of them. As she started the poem, "Away in a manger," her voice stuck in her throat, but she was able to talk louder at the end, and she did not forget a single word. Then she took a big breath.

She began as loudly as she could, "Pierre ought to stay the capital of South Dakota, but everybody will have to work hard for Pierre to keep the capital, so I say: Hurrah for Peerless Pierre for the Capital! Hurrah! Hurrah! Hurrah!"

She had thought everyone would say, "Hurrah" with her, and maybe the audience would keep on shouting for Pierre for several minutes, like a kind of applause, but at first no one made a sound.

Then some men laughed real loud laughs, and one yelled, "Did you put your girl up to that, George?"

Then everyone laughed.

Georgie edged around the organ and put her hot face on a pile of coats. She didn't want to sit in an audience where people could look at her and laugh. She had wanted so terribly to help, and all she had done was to make people laugh.

After a while, Georgie heard the superintendent call for order and invite the children to come to the tree for their sacks of candy. She didn't want to miss that treat, so she wiped her tears away on her sleeve and joined the others at the tree, looking around to see if the grown folk were still laughing at her.

They seemed to have forgotten her, so Georgie reached for her candy, murmured a "Thank you," and went back to the seat beside Mama.

Georgie was very glad that Papa was talking to some men near the door. She felt ashamed to have made such a mistake in something that was really Papa's business, and she didn't want to face him yet.

Mama squeezed her hand and asked, "What kind of candy did you get?" Georgie liked that question much better than if Mama had tried to comfort her. She was glad that the program was over, and that they could go home.

On the way home, the cold, frosty air cooled Georgie's hot face and made her feel more comfortable in her mind.

At home, Mama remarked, "This has been a big night—we'll get right into bed."

Linnie asked anxiously, "Can't I hang up my stocking?"

"Oh, of course," Mama agreed. She brought two clean stockings from the bureau drawer.

Papa tied Linnie's to the kitchen doorknob and Georgie's to the bedroom doorknob.

As Linnie stood beside the stove to be dressed for bed, she asked, "How will Santa find our stockings when we haven't any fireplace?"

Papa answered, "Oh, Santa's a smart fellow! He slides down the stovepipe and pushes open the stove door. Then he brushes the soot out of his eyes and looks around for stockings. 'Ah!' he says, 'here's one on the kitchen door. It must belong to a very good girl, or else her mama would not let her hang it on the kitchen door.' So he finds some nice gift in his bag and puts it in that girl's stocking."

This talk about stockings made Georgie uncomfortable. She had a pretty good idea who Santa was, but she wondered if, by putting her stocking in a different place from Linnie's, Papa meant that she wasn't a good-enough girl to have her stocking in the most conspicuous place.

When she had pulled on her long-legged, Canton-flannel "sleepers" over her cold feet, and had worked her way into the sleeves, she looked around for Mama to button up the back, but Mama was busy tucking Linnie into bed. She didn't want to ask Papa to help her, for fear he would have something to say about the speech she had made, but he beckoned to her, so she backed slowly up to him.

Papa's big fingers fumbled with the buttons, down the back and across. Then he turned Georgie around to face him. She felt tears in her eyes, so she put her forehead down against his vest.

"I'm sorry I made people laugh," she whispered.

Papa patted her shoulder. "I think," he said softly, "that Santa will have heard about what a shouter you are for Pierre and will put a red-satin badge in your stocking."

"Oh, Papa!" she breathed, "do you really think he will?"

"I do indeed!" Papa replied, his eyes twinkling. Then he brushed her face with a moustachey kiss.

Georgie put her arms around Papa's neck and squeezed hard. She was very glad Papa understood that she had been trying to help him.

"Merry Christmas, Papa!" she whispered and ran to Mama to say her prayers and then cuddle down in bed.

As she lay with an arm around Linnie, she dimly heard Papa say, "That Georgie! Whatever put it into her head to do that! Lucy, did you put those extra badges away somewhere?"

But she was so sleepy that what he said did not make much sense.

Chapter 7
Christmas Day

On Christmas morning Georgie woke with a shiver. Even in the dark she realized that her woolen, pieced quilt was gone, and that her feet, even inside her sleepers, were ice-cold. Linnie was gone, too.

"Linnie!" she called. "Where are you, Linnie?"

Linnie shouted from the sitting room, "Santa came, Dodo! Santa came!"

Georgie pulled the sheet from the bed and used it for a shawl as she hurried through the door. The glow from the baseburner lighted the sitting room enough so that she could see that Linnie had made a tent for herself by draping the quilt over some chairs. She could also see that the sliding doors into the parlor had been pulled shut. They were always open, unless the parlor was being used as a guest room.

"Why are the doors shut?" she asked Linnie. "Did someone come in the night?"

"Santa came!" Linnie cried, sticking her head out of her tent. "See my candy?" She waved a striped candy stick.

Georgie walked up close to the doors to look through the tiny crack where the two sides did not fit tight in the middle. "I can't see anything," she whispered to Linnie, who had tagged behind her.

Linnie put her candy cane into her mouth so that she could use her hand to feel for the little sunken ring that helped a person to pull the doors, but she couldn't reach it.

"Open them," she said to Georgie.

Georgie pulled Linnie's sticky hand away from the door. "No," she replied, "we mustn't open them without permission. But I wish I knew why they are shut. Do you suppose maybe Papa and Mama put a Christmas tree in there after we went to bed?" She tried again to peek through the crack, but it was no use.

Linnie's mouth was too full of candy for her to talk, but she tugged at Georgie's hand, pulling her to the long, bulgy stocking hanging from the bedroom door.

Georgie untied the stocking from the knob and crept with Linnie into the tent. "Nuts," she whispered, "and candy—an apple—two oranges. Papa said there'd be a badge." She reached with her fingertips down into the very toe of the stocking. "Oh! Oh! here it is!" She drew out a little roll of gilt paper.

Linnie took her candy out of her mouth. "Open it!" she demanded. Then she put the cane back in her mouth and reached for the package.

Georgie turned her shoulder to Linnie. "No!" she said, "you'll spoil it! Don't touch!" She unrolled the paper and there it was—a truly Peerless-Pierre-for-the-Capital badge, just like the one Papa wore in parades.

Linnie wiped her fingers on her sleepers and reached for it again.

"No, Linnie, no!" Georgie scolded. She pinned the beautiful badge to her own sleepers and leaned out of the tent to see it better. Even in the half-dark of the stove light the red satin and the heavy gold fringe glittered against the white flannel.

Linnie leaned around to look. "Oh! Oh!" she screamed, "I want one, too!"

"You can't," Georgie said. "I got it because I made a campaign speech. You aren't big enough." Then when she saw Linnie screwing up her face to cry, she added, "Maybe when you are nine, Papa will give you a badge, too. Do you want a piece of my candy?"

Before Linnie could answer, the sliding doors were opened, and Papa and Mama appeared, shouting, "Merry Christmas, girls!"

The girls tore out of their tent and ran to hug them, shouting, "Merry Christmas," over and over. It ended up in one of the wonderful hugging huddles that Georgie loved—Papa and Mama and Linnie and Georgie all tangled up together.

Papa said, "We'd better get this thing going before the sun comes up to spoil the effect." He pushed the sliding doors clear back and took a package of matches from his wrapper pocket.

Georgie ran past him into the parlor. "It is a Christmas tree!" she shouted.

It stood between the front windows where the Bible stand usually was kept. Its top scraped the ceiling. It was draped with ropes of cranberries and popcorn.

Georgie went up close and looked carefully at the packages tied to the branches. She had hoped for a new Christmas doll, but the packages didn't look like the shape of a doll. Then she saw them! Two dolls—sitting among the branches, their white china faces shining in the candlelight!

As the candles blazed up, Linnie saw them, too. "Dollies!" she screamed. "Dollies! Dollies!" She jumped up and down as she screamed.

Georgie didn't scream. She felt that a new doll was not something to scream about. It was something to make her take big breaths. She was so happy that she stood perfectly still, breathing deeply, while Linnie danced around her, screaming.

Papa reached around from the back of the tree where there were no candles, and took one doll down from its perch. He looked it over very carefully. "What do you suppose this thing is?" he asked.

Linnie hopped up and down, screaming, "Mine! My dolly!"

Papa looked at the note pinned on the blue dress. "For a dear little girl from Papa and Mama," he read.

Linnie kept screaming and jumping up and down. She even tried to jump up and snatch the doll from Papa.

"Not so fast, baby!" Papa said, turning the doll around and around. "We've got to find out who this dear little girl is." Finally he found another note.

"For Miss Linnie Clark," he read, and with a low bow handed the doll to Linnie.

Linnie grabbed it, and right away she sat down on the floor to take off its dress.

"That is because she is only three years old," Georgie thought, as she waited. It was wonderful to wait. She wanted to keep on having nice chills run up and down her backbone. So she stood looking up at her beautiful doll, and waited.

Papa pretended he didn't know the doll was for her. While he hunted for the note, Georgie stood with her mouth open, breathing faster and faster. Then Papa found the note. It said, "For a helpful little girl from Papa and Mama."

That word "helpful" made Georgie feel all warm and happy inside. She smiled at Mama, who sat on the floor trying to keep Linnie from pulling her doll's dress to pieces. She smiled up at Papa.

Papa's eyes were twinkling at her. "To Miss Georgiana Clark," he read. Then he handed the doll to her with a very low bow. "Sweets to the sweet," he added.

Georgie took the doll carefully in both hands. She felt of the cuddly, cloth body. She smoothed the hard china head. "See, Linnie," she said, "my doll's hair is black."

Linnie held up her doll. Its china head was painted yellow. "Shoes," Linnie said, pointing to the black boots painted on the doll's china feet.

"Mine, too," Georgie said. "My doll has a dress just like my new poplin. Thank you, Mama!" She went over to Mama and hugged and kissed her. Then she kissed Papa. "Thank you very much, Papa," she said, "for giving me the most beautiful doll in the world."

Georgie looked at her most beautiful doll for a long time, trying to decide what to name her. Not any name she could think of seemed good enough. Then she remembered that Mama had told her about the most wonderful girl in the world. She was about Georgie's age and was blind and deaf and couldn't talk, but she had learned to read. Her name was Helen Keller. So now Georgie knew what she would call her new doll.

"I'm going to name her 'Helen Keller,' " she said.

As she looked up, she saw Papa's eyebrows twitching. "That's my Georgie!" he said laughing.

Georgie was too happy to mind being laughed at.

Mama, from her place down on the floor, said, "I think that's lovely. Now do take good care of Helen Keller, won't you?"

"Oh, yes!" Georgie promised. "Who wouldn't take good care of the best doll in the world?"

Papa gave her shoulder a little pat. "Well, I guess we'll open the rest of the presents after breakfast." He snuffed out the wax candles, saying, "We don't want to leave any of these burning and maybe start a fire."

Just then Britta rang the silver bell, so they all went to the sitting room. Britta had put away the the quilt and the sheet and had rolled up the window shades, and had set the table for breakfast. The pale morning light made the silver coffee pot and the silver bell shine.

"Merry Christmas, Britta!" they all exclaimed at once.

"Merry Christmas!" Britta answered, as she placed a big platter of eggs and bacon on the table.

Georgie put Helen Keller in Papa's rocker. Linnie put her doll there, too. "She is Bessie," she told Georgie. "Helen Keller can take care of her."

After breakfast they went back into the parlor, and Papa took the rest of the presents from the tree. A new bottle of perfumery and a box of good-smelling powder were for Mama, from Papa and the girls. There were some large linen handkerchiefs embroidered with a big "G" for Papa, from Mama and the girls. There was a box of crunchy candy for everybody from Uncle Dudley Scott and Auntie Rose who lived in Chicago.

"This is from Chicago, too," Papa said, handing Georgie a big flat box.

She laid Helen Keller carefully down on the floor where she was sitting and opened the box. "Parcheesi!" she exclaimed, "from Cousin Helen Scott. I played parcheesi at Susan's once. Now Susan can play with my game. Look, Linnie, parcheesi!"

"Linnie is too little for games like that," Mama explained. "Let her play with her doll. Papa and I will play parcheesi with you when you are tired of your doll."

"I won't ever be tired of Helen Keller," Georgie said, laying the game aside and picking up her dolly.

The last two packages were more gifts from Papa and Mama. "This is a Kate Greenaway book for you, Linnie," Mama said.

"Thank you, Mama." Linnie went back to singing a lullaby to Bessie.

"This is for you." Papa turned to Georgie. She pulled off the wrapping paper and read the title, *Little Lord Fauntleroy*. She leafed through the book, looking at the pictures. "Thank you very much, Papa and Mama," she said. "Miss May said she wanted each of us to read one book before the end of the Christmas vacation. This will be my book." Then she laid the book on top of the big Bible.

"Let's play house with our dolls," she suggested to Linnie. So they played house until dinnertime, which was at noon, just as it was on Sundays.

At dinner, Britta wore a new pink-and-white-striped dress. "Thank you for the dress," she said to Mama. "Here is Merry Christmas for you and the Mister." She handed Mama a small, brown wooden box, carved and painted with red flowers. "From the old country," she explained.

"Thank you, Britta," Mama said, "we will use it to keep jewelry safe."

"Now maybe I can keep track of my cuff links and shirt studs, thanks to you, Britta," Papa added.

Georgie was glad that Britta was having a good time, along with the rest of the family.

When Linnie took her nap, Papa said, "Well, now that our baby is tucked away, how about a game of parcheesi, Georgie?" He set out the game and explained the rules to her.

Georgie asked, "There are supposed to be four players—can Helen Keller play with us?"

"Certainly," Papa answered, "if you can teach her the rules."

"I'll play for her," Georgie said, feeling a little uncomfortable because she thought Papa was making fun of her. She put her doll in a chair in front of the board. Then Mama came, and they played one game. Helen Keller beat.

"I guess that's enough for today," Papa said. "I've got to go down to the office a while, even if it is a holiday."

Then Linnie woke up from her nap, and they spent the rest of the day playing happily with their new dolls.

That night Georgie took Helen Keller and her red Pierre badge to bed with her. She told herself, "Papa wouldn't have given me the badge if he had been angry about my speech. Maybe it wasn't so bad for people to laugh at it. Anyway, I made them think about the capital. But I wish I could think of a better way to help. Maybe Helen Keller can help me."

Chapter 8
Headquarters

On the evening of January sccond, Georgie complained as she left the dinner table, "Oh, dear! Christmas vacation is nearly over, and I haven't done all the things I had planned."

"It seems to me you've had a pretty good time," Mama said. "You went to Erma Brown's birthday party, and you have been sliding every day, and Mrs. Hamilton and I took you and Susan shopping to buy goods for doll dresses."

"We were going to make lots of dresses, but we made only two—one for Susan's Prudence and one for my Helen Keller—and school begins Monday! Vacations ought to be longer."

Papa had picked up the *Pierre Daily Capital-Journal* and was reading it as he rocked in his red chair. He laid the paper down now and crooked his finger at Georgie. She walked over to him slowly.

"I suppose you will tell me to count my blessings," she began, feeling her cheeks growing hot.

"No, I was going to suggest something special," Papa replied, smiling. "How would you like to go down to my office this evening?"

"To headquarters? Oh, Papa! I'd love it!"

"How late will you keep her out?" Mama asked.

"It won't take over an hour. Mr. Hamilton and I have some letters we want to get off on the night train."

"Maybe I could help you," Georgie offered.

"Maybe you can," Papa said, his eyes twinkling. "We'll see."

Georgie thought that every time she said anything about helping Papa to get the capital, his eyes twinkled that way, "as if he was laughing at me inside," she told herself uncomfortably. "But I will help some way—I'll just show him that I can."

When Mr. Hamilton stopped his horse at the front hitching post, Papa and Georgie were waiting for him. Instead of lifting Georgie into the high buggy, Papa helped her onto the horse block and into the buggy, in the same way that he always helped Mama. Georgie liked that.

As she settled down between Mr. Hamilton and Papa, she remarked, "It feels real grownup to go places after dinner."

Mr. Hamilton laughed. "We'll have to put stones on you and Susan to keep you from growing up too fast."

"I didn't mean tall. I meant grownup enough to do things," Georgie explained.

Papa put his arm across Georgie's shoulders. "This young lady wants to be grownup enough to help in our campaign," he said.

"Well, we ought to be able to find something for her to do," Mr. Hamilton answered.

All the way to the office, Georgie hoped that he would find something really important for her to do.

After they had hung their wraps on the office hatrack, Papa gave Georgie a little paper picture book about Pierre. "You can look at this while we work," he said.

"I've seen this book," Georgie objected. "We have one at home. What is that thing?"

"It's a typewriter," Papa answered. "In an up-and-coming-Capital-Campaign office we have to have all the latest inventions. Now, no more questions!"

Georgie watched Papa and Mr. Hamilton roll letter paper into their typewriters and strike the keys to make black words appear on the paper. She felt she might burst if she couldn't ask questions about these wonderful machines, but she put her fingers over her mouth to keep from talking. "Papa might not let me help if I talk too much," she told herself.

After a while Papa pulled the paper out of his machine and reached for a tall black pen standing in a cup on his desk. He dipped the pen in an ink bottle and signed the letter.

Georgie edged up to Papa's elbow. "What makes the pen stand up?" she asked.

Papa showed her the lead pellets in the cup. "The lead shot holds the pen in place and keeps the steel point of the pen shiny," he explained. "Now please go back to your chair. If you don't bother me any more, I'll show you that talking box."

"Oh!" Georgie replied, "I will be good!"

When Papa and Mr. Hamilton had each signed several letters, Papa said, "Now I guess you can help, Georgie."

When she hurried over to him, he said, "Sit here and put each letter into its envelope, seal it, and stamp it. You'll have to look carefully at the address on the letter to be sure you put it into the right envelope."

"I'll be very careful," Georgie promised, "just like a real secretary." She sat down in the revolving chair and began to work. She thought, "I'm helping! I am really helping!"

When Papa came to the desk to sign a letter, he winked at her. Georgie liked that, but she didn't wink back. "Real secretaries don't wink at the boss," she told herself.

After a while Papa said, "Well, that's the last one, Tom."

Mr. Hamilton replied, "I have only one more after this."

"Now I guess we can take time to show you the Edison phonograph," Papa said to Georgie.

"Please!" Georgie begged, licking one more stamp.

"This is the machine." Papa uncovered a big square box.

Georgie slid out of her chair and went to stand beside him. She watched him take a wide-mouthed horn from the big bookcase and set it in place on a flat brass plate that rested on the brass rod that ran across the top of the box. Then he brought a large glass jar, poured something that looked like water into it, and showed it to Georgie.

"Metal plates hang down from the lid of the jar, and these wires come up out of the lid and are attached to the rod to make it turn," he explained.

Mr. Hamilton helped Papa to attach the wires. "This is called a galvanic battery," he told Georgie, "and it makes electricity to run the machine."

Georgie had read about Benjamin Franklin and his kite and key, but she had never seen an electrical machine. "What does the electricity do?" she asked. "I don't see any sparks the way Benjamin Franklin did."

"You won't see sparks if we hook this up right," Papa answered, "because all the spark energy will be used to make the phonograph work." He took a hollow cylinder out of a box. "This cylinder is covered with wax, and this needle fastened to the horn will make marks on the wax as someone speaks."

"What good will that do?" Georgie asked.

"Then we will run the cylinder again, and the marks in the wax will make the needle jump up and down and give out sounds through the horn."

" I don't understand," Georgie said. "Please work it so that I can see it."

"Should we waste one cylinder?" Papa asked Mr. Hamilton.

Mr. Hamilton fingered his black beard while he thought. Finally he said, "Georgie made a pretty good speech Christmas Eve. Let's have her speak it onto a cylinder. It might make a hit. Would you like that, Georgie?"

Georgie gasped, "Oh! Yes!" It was exactly what she had wanted to do, but she could hardly believe it was really happening to her.

When Georgie had practiced speaking a little bit, Mr. Hamilton said, "That will be fine." He put a cylinder onto the rod and pushed it to the left end of the rod. Then he set the brass plate, which held the needle and the horn, so that the needle rested on the wax. When the cylinder began to turn and to move toward the right end of the rod, he spoke into the horn.

"This question of where the capital is to be located affects every person in the state: boys and girls, as well as voters. The kind of life our children will live depends on the growth of South Dakota, and that growth depends on where the capital is situated. It should be in the center of the state, in a city that has access by rail, stage, and river boat, to all areas. Even little girls know that Pierre is that place. They know that Pierre is the only sensible location for the capital. I want you to hear one of them now. Georgie, you tell them!"

He pulled Georgie close to the open mouth of the horn. Georgie felt shivers run up and down her backbone. She was afraid her voice would stick in her throat the way it did sometimes when she was excited. But she took a big breath and said as loudly as she could:

"Pierre is the best place for the capital. Everybody ought to work hard for Pierre to keep the capital. So I say Hurrah for Peerless-Pierre-for-the-Capital-of-South Dakota! Hurrah! Hurrah! Hurrah!"

Mr. Hamilton then unfastened the wires, and the machine stopped. When he had pulled the cylinder back to the left end of the rod and had restarted it, his voice came out of the horn. It buzzed a good deal, and Georgie thought it was hard to understand. She was disappointed because his voice sounded so mixed up, and yet it did really sound like Mr. Hamilton's voice.

After his speech was over, there was a long, buzzing noise. "That's you, getting ready," Papa said. Then Georgie heard a high, thin, little voice saying, "Pierre is the best . . ."

"Do I sound like that?" she asked, horrified.

"Sh-h-h!" Papa warned.

After Mr. Hamilton had stopped the machine, he said, "Georgie's voice came out much clearer than mine. That tells us that high tones register best. We'd better have tenor speakers after this, instead of bass voices like mine."

Papa began to close up the phonograph. "That's right," he said. "We learned something tonight. Well —Mr. Smith is going to take this machine up to the north part of the state. The farmers there will come to see this new invention, and that will give Mr. Smith a chance to talk about Pierre. I'm glad Georgie's voice comes out so well."

"Take my speech?" Georgie cried. "Why, I thought you were just practicing!"

"Your speech—all over the state," Papa answered. "You've made quite a contribution to the campaign tonight."

Georgie was so full of pride that her chest hurt. She wanted to jump up and down, wave her arms and shout, but she thought, "A secretary who was a perfect lady would not jump around and yell," so she kept her mouth shut tight as she gathered up the letters for Papa and then put on her wraps.

All the way home her heart was singing, "I helped Pierre-for-the-Capital. I helped; I helped!" When she opened the front door, she could not keep her happiness in any longer. "Mama!" she screamed, "I made a truly campaign speech, and I am a secretary!" She ran into Mama's arms and hugged her tight, crying over and over, "I did, Mama—I talked into the phonograph, and I put the stamps on straight. I helped!"

Chapter 9
Playing Secretary

"I wish something exciting would happen," Georgie exclaimed at dinner the following Monday evening.

"You haven't settled down from the holidays yet," Mama answered.

"There will be exciting things happening around here as soon as the ground thaws," Papa said. "We're going to have a streetcar line go past our house."

"Does that mean the street will be torn up all spring?" Mama asked.

"For a few weeks, anyway. Why?"

"It won't be any use to do spring housecleaning while that is going on. When do you think they will start?" Mama asked.

"Sometime in February," Papa replied. "If they start then, the dust should be settled by the last of April."

Mama went to her desk and picked up a calendar. "I'll mark the week before Easter. Mr. Wilson, the handyman, has been asking me when I would want him to help me."

Georgie asked, "May we watch the streetcar men?"

Papa told her, "You might even make reports to me. You see, this streetcar line is going to help Pierre keep the capital, because it will make it easy for the legislators to go from their hotels to the statehouse. Huron doesn't have any streetcars."

"I would like to make some reports," Georgie said. "I'd like to write them, just like a real secretary."

"That will be fine," Papa agreed, "very business-like."

After that, Georgie watched every day for the streetcar men. On Ground-hog Day, in February, she told Papa, "The ground hog couldn't see his shadow today, because it was cloudy, so he'll stay outside his hole, and it will be spring. Does that mean the streetcar men will start work?"

"Tomorrow," Papa said.

The next evening Georgie put a note beside Papa's plate.

Pierre, South Dakota
February 3, 1890

Report
Today men mesured the street with a chane and put flags by our sidewalk.

G. Clark, Sec.

Papa wrote "measured" and "chain" above the two words Georgie had misspelled. He wrote "Surveying" at the top edge of the note and put it into his pocket.

"That is pretty good," he told Georgie, "but you'd better look up long words in the dictionary. My secretaries must know how to spell."

"Yes, sir," Georgie said. She wished she had taken time to look up those words before she gave Papa the note.

The very next day there was a snowstorm. "That shows how stupid the ground hog is," Georgie told Susan as they fought against the sleety wind on their way home from school.

Georgie was so worried that she could hardly wait for Papa to come home to ask him, "Will this spoil the streetcar work?"

"Oh, it will slow it down a little," Papa answered, holding the door open so that he could shake the snow from his coat.

"Well, I call this a real blizzard," Mama remarked, as she carried his overshoes into the kitchen to dry.

The next morning Papa said, "Mama was right. It is a blizzard." They all listened for the school bell at eight-thirty, but all they could hear was the wind howling around the house. All they could see outside was whirling snow.

When nine o'clock passed, and they had heard no school bells, Georgie shouted, "No school, Linnie! I can play all day with you! Let's make dresses for our dolls."

Mama watched Georgie making the dresses. "You cut them pretty well," she said, "but your stitches are too long." She showed Georgie how to take tiny stitches with a fine needle, so that the seam would look almost like machine sewing.

When Georgie had finished Bessie's dress, she told Linnie, "Now you leave this on Bessie! The reason Bessie never has any good clothes is because you tear them, taking them off all the time."

"Don't either!" Linnie shouted. She went into the bedroom, dragging Bessie by one arm. "I don't like Georgie!" she screamed. She stayed in the bedroom until Georgie had finished Helen Keller's dress.

Then Georgie called, "Be good, Linnie! Let's have a tea party."

"That's my peacemaker," Mama whispered softly, as she brought cookies and milk for the tea party.

"Cookies!" Linnie screamed, dragging Bessie to the doll tea table that Georgie was setting.

"What do you say to Georgie for dressing Bessie so nicely?" Mama asked.

"Thank you, Dodo. I be good now."

That evening Papa said, "Snow doesn't usually last long in February. Those men will be back in a week." And it really was only a week later when the men began again to work in front of Georgie's house.

Her report that evening stated:

Pierre, South Dakota
February 14, 1890

Report
The men are scraping the road to make it flat.

G. Clark, Sec.

P.S. This is Valentine's Day.

Under her name she drew a heart, and in it she printed: "I love you."

"Thanks for the valentine," Papa said, "but what is this 'Sec.'?"

"Mama explained it was short for 'secretary,' " Georgie replied.

"Let's hear you spell it."

"S-e-c-r-e-t-a-r-y."

"All right," Papa decided, "since you can spell it, you may write it 'sec.' I think maybe one report a week will be enough. I don't want to overwork my secretary."

Georgie's next report read:

Pierre, South Dakota
February 28, 1890

Report

The men have taken our dirt across Huron Street and have dumped it in the next block. Are they doing it right?

G. Clark, Sec.

Papa explained, "Capitol Avenue must be made level—not up high at Center Street, low at our corner, and up again at Pierre Street."

He marked the report "Grading," and put that note also in his pocket.

A week later Georgie's report said:

Pierre, South Dakota
March 7, 1890

Report

The men took away our sidewalk and cut close to our fence. Will it tumble down?

G. Clark, Sec.

Papa wrote "Grading Continued" on the note. He said, "The fence won't tumble down if we build a retaining wall."

"What is that?" Georgie asked.

"A stone wall to keep the dirt from crumbling away under the fence."

Georgie wanted to ask more questions, but Papa went out in such a hurry that she decided just to watch the workmen.

The next week she wrote:

Pierre, South Dakota
March 14, 1890

Report

Some men brought pretty stones and built our wall. The streetcar men aren't working in our block any more. May I sit on the courthouse steps and watch them?

G. Clark, Sec.

Papa's eyebrows went up when he read the report. He handed it to Mama.

Mama read it and exclaimed, "Mercy no! Ladies don't sit around in public places!"

"Then I suppose that is my last report," Georgie complained. "I like to make reports."

"I'm going to have another little job for you," Papa said, "about the time you find a pasqueflower."

After that, Georgie and Linnie hunted for pasqueflowers every afternoon after school. Twice there were snowstorms, so they couldn't hunt, but almost every day they went to the hill across the street, where they had gone sliding in the winter.

One day Linnie brought a furry, green leaf to Georgie. "You said it was a kitty kind of flower," she said, "and this is a kitty leaf."

"Oh, Linnie! That is truly a pasqueflower leaf!" Georgie cried. "Where did you find it?" She followed Linnie to the other side of the hill.

"There!" Linnie pointed.

Georgie knelt down by the clump of silver-green fuzzy leaves. "Right in the middle," she showed

Linnie, "is a little gray bud. When it opens, it will be a pasqueflower, and we will take it to Papa."

The next day, as soon as Georgie came home from school, they hurried to the hill.

"See, Linnie, it's open!" Georgie cried.

Linnie put the tip of her finger softly on the furry, lavender petal. "Kitty!" she exclaimed.

Georgie carefully picked the pasqueflower and took it home and put it in a blue-glass cinderella slipper vase.

That evening, she put the vase beside Papa's plate on top of a note.

Pierre, South Dakota
April 10, 1890

Report
I am ready for the new job.
G. Clark, Sec.

"What's this about a job?" Papa asked, when he read the note.

"You said you'd have a job for me when I found a pasqueflower," Georgie reminded him.

"Oh, that! Oh, yes! Well, I just meant that the weather must be fairly warm for this job. I guess if the wild flowers are out, it's time to go ahead with it.

I've been talking with Mama about making some sketches for our new campaign booklet. I thought maybe you could help her by carrying her easel and taking care of Linnie while she sketched."

That kind of job didn't sound to Georgie much like a secretary's job, but she didn't want Papa to know how disappointed she felt, so she answered in her most grownup voice, "I'll be glad to help Mama."

"Do you still think you want the view from the Island?" Mama asked Papa. "It seems such a long way to go for such a little picture."

"It's the only place from which you can see how Pierre is built up on ledges back from the river. Cameras don't show it well. The whole committee wants you to sketch it from the Island."

"Well," Mama answered, "this next Saturday will be the best time. I plan to clean house next week, so as to be through with that job by Easter."

Georgie took Linnie into the under-the-porch house. "This is a very important job," she began, "and you will have to help by not crying or saying you want to go home in the middle of it."

"I'll be good if I can take Bessie," Linnie agreed.

"I'll take Helen Keller, too, but we won't play with dolls if Mama needs us to help. Remember, Linnie!"

On Saturday, right after breakfast, Georgie helped Mama load the buggy with her easel and drawing materials, and a big basket of lunch that Britta had made. Linnie came out with the two dolls and a big spoon for digging sand.

Then Papa helped them into the buggy, and they were off!

When they reached the office, Papa gave Mama the reins. "Georgie, you help Mama," he said, "because she's going to have her hands pretty full." Then he lifted his hat, called "Good-by," and went into his office.

Mama took the reins in both hands. "Sit tight, now, girls. And Georgie, you hang onto Linnie." She clucked to Harry and drove toward the river.

At the bridge she pulled Harry to a stop.

"Oh! We're going on the bridge!" Georgie cried.

They sat a few minutes, watching the boats that held up the bridge swing out and back, up and down, as the water moved them.

"I don't see anyone coming from Fort Pierre," Mama said, "so I suppose we might as well get started. Papa says the bridge is wide enough for teams to pass, but I don't want to have to try that."

Georgie thought, too, that the bridge looked too narrow for passing, but she tried to be brave. "There isn't anyone coming," she told Mama.

Mama drew the reins tight and clucked at Harry. Georgie saw that the end of the bridge rested on the riverbank and did not move when Harry stepped onto it. Then the buggy rolled onto the planks that rested on the boats. The plank roadway moved up and down with the boats as Harry put his feet down carefully and lifted them quickly.

"Mama!" Georgie shouted, "the bridge goes away from Harry's feet!"

"Hang onto Linnie," Mama answered.

Harry pointed his ears forward and put his head down. "He pulls so hard!" Mama gasped.

"Don't drive into the water, Mama!" Linnie screamed.

"Hush, Linnie! You'll scare Harry!" As Georgie tightened her right arm around Linnie's waist, she felt Helen Keller slipping out of her left hand. "Now, see what you've done!" she scolded. "You made Helen Keller fall!"

"I'm scared!" Linnie sobbed. "I want to go home!"

"Don't be such a baby!" Georgie told her, but in her heart she wanted to go home, too. She shut her eyes and waited for the bridge to break, or for Harry to jump off into the water.

Then the clop-clop of Harry's shoes on the planks stopped. Georgie opened her eyes. They had come off the bridge onto the sandy island. Harry had slowed down and was edging off the road.

Mama climbed down over the wheel and tied Harry to a little willow tree, just as if nothing had happened. She said, "Georgie, will you please help Linnie down and bring me my box of crayons?"

When Mama had set up her easel, put the pad of drawing paper on it, and opened her crayon box, she told the two girls, "Now, please don't bother me about anything. I'm sure, Georgie, you can manage Linnie by yourself."

Georgie helped Linnie to build sand castles big enough for the dolls to sit in.

"Really," she explained, "we have to put the dolls in the basements, because we can't keep the house walls from caving in."

Linnie thought it was fun to see the walls cave in, and sometimes she even knocked them down on purpose.

When it seemed to Georgie that she had been amusing Linnie for a very long time, Mama came over to look at the castles. "They are very fine," she said, "but now let's have lunch."

Georgie lugged the picnic basket from the buggy and helped Mama spread a cloth on the sand.

As they ate Britta's good deviled eggs, ham sandwiches, and elegantly frosted chocolate cake, Georgie tried to talk in a grownup way with Mama, the way a real secretary would.

"Is this the island Lewis and Clark camped on when they came up the river with Sacajawea?" she inquired.

"I think that was Farm Island, below here," Mama told her, pouring Linnie some milk from the quart jar. "This island was probably just a sand bar then. But how do you know about Lewis and Clark?"

"Miss May read us a story about Sacajawea," Georgie answered. "Please, may I have another piece of cake?"

"Sacajawea was a remarkable young woman," Mama said, handing over a big chunk of cake. "Here's some more milk to go with it," she added, filling Georgie's cup.

After they had eaten all they could, Georgie helped Mama put the dishes into the basket. Then she took Linnie far enough away from the easel so that they wouldn't bother Mama.

"You can be Sacajawea," she said to Linnie,

"and I will be Lewis-and-Clark, and the dolls can be soldiers."

They had so much fun playing at being explorers that Georgie was sorry when Mama told them she was ready to go home.

"How do you like my picture?" Mama asked, as she gathered up her crayons.

Georgie walked over to the easel. "I can tell which is the statehouse and which is the courthouse, but the rest is pretty fuzzy," she said honestly.

"Well, that's the way Papa said to make it," Mama replied. "Let's get the things into the buggy."

When they were all in, Mama clucked at Harry. "Giddap, Harry! Giddap!" She had to urge him this time to step from the sand onto the bridge.

Georgie put her arms around Linnie, who was puckering her face to cry. "Remember, you are Sacajawea," she said. "She was never afraid of anything."

Harry didn't seem to mind the bridge after he was on it. He clopped pretty fast, and the bridge went up and down, but Linnie stopped being scared and clapped her hands along with Georgie. "We'll keep time to Harry's feet," Georgie said, trying to match every clop with a handclap.

The trip home seemed much shorter than the

trip to the Island. "I had a very good time," Georgie told Mama, as they unpacked the buggy. "I'd like to do it again."

When Papa came home, he looked at all the sketches. "You did a fine piece of work, Lucy. I think we can use all these sketches in our publicity."

Before she went to bed, Georgie gave Papa this report:

Pierre, South Dakota
April 12, 1890

Report
I helped Mama make pictures for the Capital Committee. Mama did the drawing.
G. Clark, Sec.

Papa wrote "Publicity" on this note, before he tucked it into his vest pocket.

Chapter 10
Spring Housecleaning

"It isn't time to get up yet," Georgie argued the following Monday morning, as she tried to roll away from Britta's hand on her shoulder. "I want to finish a nice dream I was having."

"Your mama said 'get up,'" Britta insisted. "Housecleaning today."

Georgie opened her eyes wide and sat up. She shook Linnie, who was curled up next to the wall. "Get up, Linnie! It's housecleaning! Where is Mama, Britta?"

Britta, hurrying out into the sitting room, turned around long enough to answer, "Mama is talking to man. You dress Linnie today."

"What's housecleaning?" Linnie asked, as Georgie helped her with her pantywaist.

"Don't you remember housecleaning last fall, when they set up the stoves? It's fun, Linnie. I wish I could stay home and help."

"I'll help," Linnie agreed, twisting away from Georgie, "and I can put on my own dress."

"I'll button it for you," Georgie offered, hurrying into her own clothes.

When Linnie was buttoned, she ran out without waiting for Georgie.

Georgie dressed herself carefully, so that she would look nice in school. When she was ready and went into the sitting room, she was surprised to find that the breakfast table was not set. So she went to the kitchen to look for Britta.

"You eat here," Britta told her, pointing to a bowl of oatmeal and a pitcher of cream on the kitchen table. "Only two spoons of sugar," she added, as Georgie reached for the sugar bowl.

"Where are Papa and Mama and Linnie?" Georgie asked, dipping into her cereal.

Britta laughed. "The Mister, he ate fast and said he'd get out of way quick. That Linnie–she ate already and gone with Mama in back shed."

"You think housecleaning is funny, don't you?" Georgie asked, rolling the good oatmeal on her tongue. "I think it's nice."

Britta faced Georgie and put her hands on her hips, with her elbows sticking out. "I like clean house, ya, but it's hard work for your mama and me. Men and little girls . . ." She raised one arm and waved it at the door—"Out!"

"I'm not a little girl any more, Britta. When I get back from school, I'm going to help."

Then Mama and the handyman came in from the back shed, with Linnie tagging along behind.

"Georgie, you remember Mr. Wilson who helps us to clean," Mama said, turning toward the man.

Georgie slid out of her chair. "Good morning, Mr. Wilson," she said.

She noticed that Mr. Wilson had on a blue cotton shirt and denim pants, instead of the wool pants and heavy sweater he had worn when he helped to houseclean in the fall.

He ducked his gray head toward Georgie, as he asked, "Are you going to hold my hammer for me again?"

"I have to go to school at eight-thirty," Georgie replied, very much pleased that Mr. Wilson remembered how she had helped him, "but I could help until then."

"I'll help!" Linnie cried, peeking around from behind Mama.

"I think Mr. Wilson can do better without help right now. When the carpet has been cleaned and tacked down again, maybe you girls can help to set the furniture back. Now Georgie, please get your jacket and also Linnie's, and take her out to the swing or somewhere until the school bell rings."

Georgie thought how much more fun it was to do grownup things, such as holding hammers for Mr. Wilson and being a secretary for Papa. "Taking care of Linnie is a baby job!" she muttered under her breath as she started for the front hall and the two jackets.

Then she realized that she had talked loud enough for Mama to hear.

Mama followed Georgie to the hall and put her arm across her shoulders. "This is part of getting the capital," she explained. "The chairman of the committee must have a nice, clean house to make him feel happy. Then he can do better work for

Pierre. And I can't houseclean with Linnie under my feet every minute. If you amuse her outside of school hours, you will be helping Papa get the capital."

"Oh!" Georgie exclaimed. "I just thought how tiresome it is to play baby games all the time. I'll be a good helper. I will, truly." She kissed Mama and ran out to the kitchen, calling, "Let's swing, Linnie!" In her mind, she was thinking, "There are certainly some very tiresome ways to help Papa get the capital."

When Georgie came home at noon, the lunch was set in the kitchen, and the sitting room was empty. Even the carpet was gone.

"Papa won't be home until evening," Mama said, "so we will just hurry through a bite of lunch."

When Georgie crammed the last bit of cooky into her mouth, Mama asked her, "Do you think you could get Linnie to sleep before you go back to school?"

"I guess so," Georgie answered, swallowing the cooky fast. "Come on, Linnie, it's time for your nap."

Linnie screamed, "I want Mama to rock me," and she tried to pull away from Georgie's hand. But Georgie coaxed. "You play you are a mama and put your Bessie to sleep, and I'll put Helen Keller to sleep."

She took off Linnie's shoes and boosted her gently onto the bed.

Linnie curled up with Bessie in her arms. "Sing 'Rockaby,' " she said.

Georgie lay down beside Linnie with Helen Keller between them, and sang lullabies until she heard the school bell. When she peeked at Linnie, she saw that her eyes were shut, so she tiptoed out of the bedroom, picked her way over the bare, dusty floor of the sitting room, and went outdoors to find Mama.

"Linnie is asleep, and I'm going," she told Mama, who was standing with Mr. Wilson in the back yard. She saw that the sitting-room carpet was thrown over the clothesline, and that Mr. Wilson held two rattan carpet beaters, one in each hand, swinging first one beater and then the other.

"Thank you, dear," Mama said. "You are a good helper."

Mr. Wilson began to beat the carpet before Georgie could get clear out of his way. The dust went up her nose and made her sneeze. She could still smell it when she caught up with Susan at the next corner.

"I can smell that awful dust clear to here," she said to Susan.

"We are going to houseclean when Mr. Wilson is through at your place," Susan said, adding, "I hate housecleaning."

"I like housecleaning, except the dust," Georgie remarked, blowing her nose hard on her handkerchief.

When Georgie reached home at four o'clock, Linnie danced along the sidewalk to meet her. "I helped!" she shouted, as she caught Georgie's hand, and they ran together into the house. "I'm going to help, too," Georgie panted, all out of breath.

"You are just in time," Mama began. "We need all the shovers we can get."

Georgie remembered how she had helped to shove when they put the carpet down in the fall. "Which side of the carpet is already tacked?" she asked.

"The bedroom side," Mama answered, so Georgie took Linnie's hand and stood on that edge of the carpet, close to the bedroom door.

Britta stood on the edge at the kitchen corner, and Mama stood at the parlor corner. Mr. Wilson stood on the bare floor at the bay window and pulled the carpet toward himself.

"We've got to make the carpet tight enough so that the rocking chair will move on it when we rock," Georgie explained to Linnie.

"Now shove!" Mr. Wilson ordered. They all pushed the carpet with their feet, toward Mr. Wilson, trying to make it fit tight and smooth.

"I guess that's as tight as we can make it now," Mr. Wilson said, when they were close to him. "Stand still, now, until I put in some tacks to hold it."

When he had hammered in a few tacks, he stood alongside Georgie and Linnie, and they all shoved again right up to the bay window. They shoved so hard that Mr. Wilson had to take out the tacks and fold the edge of the carpet under some more before he tacked it to stay.

"While Mr. Wilson is finishing the tacking," Mama said, "we might as well bring in the furniture. Is it ready, Britta?"

"Yes, ma'am," Britta answered. "I dusted the pictures and put that oil and vinegar on the wood things." She led the way to the kitchen, adding, "I think it looks good!"

Georgie and Linnie brought in the chairs, all shiny from their polishing. Then Mama asked Georgie, "Will you please bring me the pictures—just one at a time."

Georgie brought the gold-framed picture of a cupid driving a team of butterflies. She watched Mama get on the stepladder, holding her long skirt away from her feet as she climbed. Mama felt in the wall for the right hole, and then she pushed in a little nail. Then she hung the picture. "Is it straight?" she asked Georgie.

Georgie squinted to try to decide whether the bottom edge was level. "I think the right corner is a little up," she said. As she watched Mama straighten it, she added, "I just love that picture!"

Then she brought the picture that Mama had painted of yellow roses spilling out of a basket, and also the big painted photograph of cherry trees in Japan. "They are all so pretty," Georgie sighed, as she handed up the last one, "that I never can decide which one I like best."

Then Britta called, "Georgie, you hold tacks for the shelf?" So Georgie helped Britta tack the red felt drapery to the edge of the clock shelf. As she handed up the tacks, one by one, she patted the circles of pale blue satin, painted with robins on their nest, that decorated the drapery.

"Careful, now, Georgie," Mama warned her. "That's done with watercolors and may rub off." So Georgie pulled her finger away quickly. "It feels so pretty," she explained to Mama. "May I bring the clock now?"

"No, that's too heavy, but you may bring the photographs."

As Mama set the clock in place and then reached for the photographs that Georgie held up to her, Georgie looked at the framed picture of Papa and Mama in their wedding clothes, and at the hand-tinted picture of herself holding Linnie, when Linnie was a tiny baby.

"We are a pretty good-looking family, aren't we?" she remarked.

"Handsome is as handsome does," Mama answered. "Don't ever forget that, Georgie."

Then Georgie heard the front door open and Papa saying, "Well! Well!" She ran to him as he stood in the doorway, looking into the sitting room.

"Isn't it nice?" she asked. "Come, Papa, look!" She dragged him into the middle of the sitting room.

Mama and Linnie came to stand beside them. Mr. Wilson and Britta rose from the corners where they had been on their knees tacking the carpet.

"How much roomier it is with the stove out," Papa remarked.

"You say that every spring," Mama answered, smiling, "but it does look nice and clean, doesn't it?"

"It even smells clean," Papa answered.

"Does a clean house really make it easier to do the capital work?" Georgie asked him.

"It certainly does," Papa said, reaching to squeeze Mama's hand, "and I expect you did your share for the capital today." He smiled at Georgie.

"I tried," Georgie said, "but it didn't seem like real secretary work."

On Friday afternoon she wrote her report:

Pierre, South Dakota
April 18, 1890

Report
I helped houseclean all week. Is that really Pierre-for-the-Capital work?

G. Clark, Sec.

Papa marked the report "Special Duty." After he had put the note in his pocket, he added, "Everything helps!"

Chapter 11
Easter

"We finished housecleaning just in time for our Easter vacation," Georgie remarked at dinner on Friday evening.

"That's good," Mama said. "Then you'll be at hand to try on dresses. Mrs. Larson is coming next week to do the spring sewing."

"I need some new dresses," Georgie said. "I tore this one on the swing today. Can I help to sew?"

"Maybe," Mama answered. "We'll see."

"Georgie, Mr. Hamilton brought a note to the office for you," Papa said, as he handed her a pretty pink envelope.

Georgie read the note aloud. "Dear Georgie," it said. "Our Sunday-School class will decorate the church for Easter. I'll be driving by for you on Saturday morning at ten. Wear old clothes. Your teacher, Mrs. Hamilton."

"Oh, goody!" she cried. "I just love to pick flowers!"

At nine o'clock the next morning, Georgie was sitting on the horse block at the front gate, looking up the street to the Hamilton gate, where the Hamilton horse stood, hitched to a surrey.

Linnie came out and sat beside Georgie. "I'm going to pick flowers, too," she said.

"This is just Mrs. Hamilton's class," Georgie explained. "You are in Miss May's class. Mrs. Hamilton is untying her horse, now. Run in, Linnie."

"I'm going!" Linnie shouted. "I'm going to pick flowers!"

"Mama! Mama!" Georgie shouted. "Please take her in!"

Mama came out and picked Linnie up in her arms. She winked at Georgie. "We big folks will stay home, Linnie."

Georgie winked back. "Just little boys and girls are going," she said, feeling very grownup to have Mama joke with her like that.

When Mrs. Hamilton stopped to pick up Georgie, Susan called, "Sit back here with us, Georgie!"

So Georgie squeezed into the back seat with Susan, Erma, and Amy. She saw that the twins were sitting in the front seat. They turned around and said, "Hello, Georgie!" and she called back, "Hello!"

Mrs. Hamilton said, "This is all of the class that can go. We'll go down to the park and see what flowers we can find. Now, sit still, all of you."

When they reached the river end of Pierre Street, Mrs. Hamilton announced, "I'm going to the park past the bridge. How many of you have seen the bridge?"

"I helped Mama drive on it," Georgie replied.

"What was it like?" Erma asked.

"It wiggled up and down and scared Harry."

"Well, here it is," Mrs. Hamilton said, "but I'm not going to drive on it."

"Can we get out and walk on it?" Richard asked.

"Well, just a minute," Mrs. Hamilton agreed. "Whoa! Whoa, there!"

When the horse stopped, they all jumped from the surrey and ran onto the bridge.

"Let's make it jiggle!" Charles exclaimed, jumping up and down.

"We aren't heavy enough to jiggle it," Richard said, but he jumped up and down, too.

"A team is coming," Mrs. Hamilton called. "Come out of their way!" So they all climbed back into the surrey, and the Smith twins argued all the way to the park about how the bridge could be jiggled.

At the park, Mrs. Hamilton tied her horse to a tree. "We'll separate and scout around a little. Be sure to pick buds instead of wide-open flowers. The buds will be open by sermon time tomorrow."

The boys ran ahead, but Erma and Susan declared, "We are going over to those plum bushes!"

Mrs. Hamilton said, "All right, but currant and chokecherry will be nice, too," as she followed them.

Amy caught Georgie's hand, saying, "I love wild currant best."

"Me, too," Georgie agreed. "It's so spicy! I see some down by the river."

As they picked their way through the long grass left from the year before, watching carefully for snakes and avoiding the prickly rosebushes, Amy suddenly gave out a loud scream.

"Look!" she cried. "He'll be killed!"

Georgie looked where Amy pointed. There was Richard at the very top of a big cottonwood tree. He waved at them, calling, "I can see better up here!"

"Come down!" Amy screamed. "You'll fall!"

Georgie thought, "Amy gets so scared because she is only in the third grade." But she said aloud, "I think he'll get down all right."

Then she caught her own breath just in time to keep from screaming, as she saw Charles swing out on a grapevine that grew on that same tree.

She watched him swing out and back twice before his foot caught in a crotch, and he let go of the vine. "Oh! Those twins!" she cried. "They just don't have any sense at all."

"They'll probably get killed some day," Amy agreed. Then she let go Georgie's hand and broke into a run. "There are the currants!" she screamed.

Georgie ran after her and buried her face in the currant bushes glowing with spicy-sweet yellow blossoms. Then she carefully chose the best stems and broke those off.

When both girls had their arms full, Amy said, "I'm going to find Mrs. Hamilton."

"I think I'll go to the surrey," Georgie replied, "because I can't carry any more."

When she reached the surrey and had laid her flowers on the floor under the back seat, she sat on the surrey step, swinging her feet in the long grass. A meadowlark trilled near by.

"Where are you, little bird?" she called, standing up and moving carefully toward the singer. "I don't want to hurt you, birdie," she murmured softly, when she saw him swaying on a dried sunflower stalk. "Sing some more for me!" But he flew away.

Then she heard Mrs. Hamilton calling, "Oh, there you are, Georgie! Such a time as I've had rounding everyone up!"

When they were all safely back in the surrey and riding out of the park, Mrs. Hamilton told them, "When we reach the church, you will find vases on the floor of the entry, and water in the hydrant in the next yard. Each one is to arrange his own vases."

Almost before the horse had time to stop, they all hurried out of the surrey with their flowers. When Georgie had hers arranged, she asked Mrs. Hamilton, "Is that all right?"

"Your arrangements are very nice," Mrs. Hamilton commented.

"It's all so pretty," Georgie said, "and smells so sweet!"

"That's the way a church should be on Easter Sunday," Mrs. Hamilton replied, as she patted Georgie's shoulder. "Come, boys and girls! It's time to go home!"

When Georgie reached home, she took Linnie and Bessie and Helen Keller into the under-the-porch house to tell them all about her trip to the park. "I saved some flowers for you, Linnie," she said, as she gave her a sprig of currant. "You'll see tomorrow how pretty the church looks."

When Linnie woke up from her nap that afternoon, Britta called the girls into the kitchen and gave Georgie a bowl of red and blue dyed eggs, and also a box of little birds and flowers cut from gilt paper. Each piece had glue on the back like that on stamps.

"You girls fix eggs," she said, "like in the old country."

"Oh! Oh!" Linnie screamed, clapping her hands. "Easter eggs!" The girls sat at the kitchen table and decorated the eggs. When Britta had put them away, she said, "Surprise for Easter dinner. Don't tell!"

"We won't!" both girls promised. Georgie added, "Thank you, Britta."

The next day in church, Papa chose a row of seats so close to the pulpit that Georgie was seated directly in front of her own flowers. All through the service she could smell the faint plum perfume and the spicy currant. When the congregation stood to sing "Hallelujah! Christ Arose!" she sang as loudly

as she could, because she was happy that it was Easter Day and that she had helped to make the service lovely.

On Monday, when Mrs. Larson came to sew, Georgie was very much pleased to find that she was to have a brown-and-white striped dress with white collar and cuffs. "Brown looks more like an office dress than blue does," she told Mama.

"Yes?" Mama exclaimed. "Well, anyway, Mrs. Larson will do better work if you can keep Linnie out of her way."

"May I have Susan to help me?"

"You and Susan may run back and forth between your yards if you'll always let Britta or me know where you are, and if you won't bother Mrs. Hamilton."

Georgie could hardly wait to say, "Thank you, Mama," before finding Linnie. "We're going to play with Susan," she told her, "and you are to be a very good girl at Susan's."

"I like Susan," Linnie replied, tugging at Georgie's hand. "Let's go!" So they played dolls at Susan's until lunchtime. When they left, Georgie said, "It's your turn to come to our house tomorrow, Susan."

The next day they all three played "squat tag" and "tree tag" in Georgie's yard, because those were games that Linnie knew.

On Wednesday, as they played at Susan's, the Smith twins passed on their tricycle. Richard was pedaling and Charles was riding behind him.

"Please, let us ride a little," Susan begged.

"All right," Charles agreed. "You can stand behind Richard, if Georgie will play marbles with me."

After that, they took turns playing marbles and riding until they heard Britta call, "Georgie! Linnie! Lunch!"

"Come to our house tomorrow and fly kites with us," Richard called back, as the twins started home.

"We will! We promise!" the girls shouted after him. Then Susan said, "I know how to make kites. Let's make some this afternoon."

The rest of the vacation week they flew kites in the big open space where the Smith and the Clark back yards came together. Even Linnie ran up and down the grass with her little kite.

On Saturday, Mama asked Georgie to try on her new dress. "It looks like a secretary's dress," Georgie remarked, as she stood in front of Mama's big mirror. "May I wear it when I make my reports?"

"That is a good idea," Mama agreed, "and it will be a good school dress, too." Then she turned to Mrs. Larson. "It fits perfectly. Our sewing has really gone very well."

"That's because your nice girls don't bother us when we sew," the seamstress replied.

Mama winked at Georgie, and Georgie winked back.

Georgie smoothed down the front of her new secretary dress and sat down at Mama's desk to write her report.

> Pierre, South Dakota
> April 26, 1890
>
> Report
>
> Susan and I took care of Linnie all vacation week. I don't think it was real secretary work, because we had so much fun.
>
> G. Clark, Sec.

When Papa saw it, he said, "You are a very good secretary," and then added "Special Assignment" on the top edge.

"I have an office dress now. I would like to do some office work," Georgie said, and smiled happily when Papa answered, "Later on, I think maybe there will be some for you to do."

Chapter 12
Decoration Day

The day that school let out, Miss May made a speech.

"Please pack up everything in your desks and take it home. Tomorrow is Decoration Day, and the boys and girls in this room will be in the parade. The girls will wear white dresses; the boys will wear their Sunday suits. Be in front of the courthouse steps by nine o'clock, and I will tell you what to do. Now, mind! Tomorrow! Nine o'clock! Sunday clothes!"

At half-past eight the following morning, Mama was buttoning Georgie's last summer's white Sunday dress. "A pink sash isn't right for a Decoration Day Parade," Georgie said. "I wish I had a red-white-and-blue sash."

"How would this do?" Mama asked, tying a strip of bunting around Georgie's waist.

"That's more patriotic," Georgie agreed. "Now may I have a flag to carry?"

"Here," Papa said, handing her a small flag. "I bought some new ones yesterday, so we'd have flags with a star for South Dakota."

"Oh, I like that!" Georgie exclaimed, dancing out the front door.

The first thing she saw was a big flag floating from one of the porch pillars. "Oh, Papa!" she exclaimed, "you bought a new house flag! How elegant!"

"A good American can't have too many flags!" Papa called from the doorway.

Georgie waved good-by and hopped, skipped and jumped the block to the courthouse. She found Miss May standing in front of the steps, talking to her grade. "When the band begins to play, get into line behind me and keep time while you march."

Susan came up to Georgie, and they stood together watching the parade assemble.

"That's the Grand Army of the Republic." Susan pointed to some men wearing blue uniforms and funny-looking caps with a slope to the crown.

"I know," Georgie said. "They are heroes!"

Then the Women's Relief Corps fell into line. "They are the wives of the old soldiers," Susan told her.

"I like the way they swing when they march, just like the men," Georgie replied. "I wish I could see the band better—the speakers' carriage gets in my way!" She began to jump up and down to try to catch glimpses of the band. Then the carriage moved to one side, and she could see the red uniforms and the bright brass horns.

"Oh! There's Papa!" Susan cried.

Directly in front of Miss May a carriage was getting into the parade line. In it were Georgie's papa and the rest of the Capital Committee. Georgie saw that they all wore their campaign badges. She wished she had thought to wear hers.

Then the band began to play. The big drum went, "Boom!" and the little drum went, "Rat-a-tat-tat!" As the line straightened, Georgie could see the drum major in his tall bearskin hat, marching backward and waving his baton.

"What does he do that for?" Susan asked.

"Papa says he uses his baton to show the band whether to play fast or slow."

"What if he stepped on a stone, walking backward like that," Susan asked. "Do you suppose the others would march right over him?"

That idea gave Georgie the creepy chills. She hoped he wouldn't fall down, going backward down the steep slope of Pierre Street.

"Mark time!" Miss May called. Georgie heard the boys behind her shuffle their feet as they got into line and the girls giggle. She and Susan stood close behind Miss May and marked time as they did in school at dismissal time.

"March!" Miss May called. She carried the big flag that belonged to the classroom. Her long white skirt dipped into the dust at each step.

The wind blew Georgie's hair into her eyes and fluttered the flag she carried.

The fifth-sixth-grade teacher behind them also called, "Mark time!" Georgie heard the fifth and sixth grades pounding their feet on the sidewalk. The teacher then called, "March!" So they marched with a rush that crowded Georgie's grade.

Far in the rear, the seventh-eighth-grade teacher called, "Mark time!" Then Georgie knew that the whole line was marching. Her heart swelled with pride—pride in the parade, pride in Pierre, and pride in the flag of her country! It was wonderful to be a part of the Decoration Day Parade!

The parade marched down Pierre Street to Dakota Avenue, where a platform had been erected in the middle of the street, and draped with red-white-and-blue bunting, and with flags at each corner.

On the platform there was a table and some chairs. The mayor, the minister, and the governor, who was also the speaker, sat beside the table on the platform. The Capital Committee sat behind them.

Georgie watched the old soldiers and their wives sit down on the chairs beside the platform on one side, and the band take chairs on the other side of the platform.

When Miss May reached the platform, she put her flag in a flag rest nailed to the platform. Then she waved to her grade to show the boys and girls that they could go where they pleased.

Georgie and Susan moved over to the sidewalk where their mamas stood. Linnie let go Mama's hand as Georgie came up, and then sat beside her big sister on the edge of the sidewalk. Georgie helped her to turn up her skirt and sit on her panties, the way she and Susan did, so as not to get their Sunday dresses soiled.

The governor made a very long speech, and when he finally stopped, Georgie was very glad to stand up to sing. While they sang "The Star-Spangled Banner," Georgie waved her flag as fast as she could.

Then Papa came over to them and took them down a side street where Mama had tied Harry. They drove away out the east side of town, farther even than the Wells House, which was the new hotel on the far edge of town. Georgie saw that many other buggies and surreys were going along, too, in a sort of parade that wound around among the hills until they came to one hill that had tall gravestones on it. There Papa tied Harry to the fence.

Papa and Mama took some flags from under the seat; also branches of lilac, chokecherry, and plum blossoms.

They put the flowers and flags against the gravestones. While they decorated the graves, Georgie walked around the edge of the graveyard where she found a gumbo lily. She carried it to Mama, admiring the white satin petals and the chains of golden pollen as she went. "Here is a pretty one," she said. "Do you want to put it on a grave?"

"Here is a grave of a man that nobody knows," Papa pointed. "His folks must have left here a long time ago. There is no one to decorate his grave, but he was an old soldier—it says so on the stone. Let's put your lily here."

Georgie laid the beautiful white blossom on the grave, close to the stone. She found a spike of waxy yucca to go with it, and then added a purple lilac branch. Next, she put her flag into the sod to keep watch over the flowers. She felt very glad that she could decorate that old soldier's grave.

On the way home, Papa began to sing as soon as they got off the stony, winding road. All of them joined in, singing the "Battle Hymn of the Republic," "Tenting Tonight," and "Columbia, the Gem of the Ocean." Georgie loved to hear Papa's rich baritone voice, accompanied by Mama's high soprano.

She loved Decoration Day.

As they were hanging up their hats, after they reached home, Papa remarked, "The streetcars ought to be coming past here in a few days. You girls will have fun watching them."

"Do you want me to report about it?" Georgie asked him.

"Most certainly."

Chapter 13
Indian Dancers

"Papa was mistaken about the streetcars coming in a few days," Georgie remarked to Mama, after watching for them for a whole week.

"They'll be coming," Mama promised. "Just watch!" But it was the middle of June before they finally arrived.

Linnie saw them first. "Dodo!" she called, "the cars are coming!" Georgie rushed to the side porch where Linnie was standing, and the two watched the two big, gray mules pull a yellow streetcar past their house.

After that, whenever they heard a loud, squeaking noise, they knew that the car was turning onto

Capitol Avenue at Center Street, and they ran to the side yard to watch.

A week later, Papa asked them at dinner, "How would you all like to ride on the streetcars to a show that the Capital Committee is putting on downtown?"

"I would!" screamed Linnie.

"Not if you are going to scream like that," Papa said.

Linnie put both hands over her mouth. "I want to go," she said, softly.

"That's better. How about it, Mama? Would you like to take a ride on the newest streetcars in South Dakota?"

"I think it would be delightful," Mama replied.

"We will stand on the front porch and watch, Mama, so we won't miss the car," Georgie offered, after Mama had brushed their hair and set their hats neatly on their heads.

After they had been watching for what seemed a long time, Georgie spied the yellow car far up the street.

"It's coming, Papa," she called, as she took Linnie's hand and started for the front gate.

Papa and Mama caught up with the two girls at the corner. "We'll have to stand in the middle of the street to stop the car," Papa said, as he led the three out to the tracks. When the car came quite close to them, he waved at the driver.

The driver stopped the car, and Papa helped Mama up the steps, and Georgie helped Linnie. Then they were on their way. Georgie watched Papa put the fares into a glass box near the driver.

When Georgie screwed around on the seat to look at the other passengers, she almost fell off. "These straw seats are awfully slippery," she complained to Papa.

"Rattan, not straw," Papa replied, "and grownup secretaries don't squirm."

"I'm sorry," Georgie apologized, thinking that it had been a long time since she had been given any secretary work .

The streetcar screeched around the curve at Center Street and started down the long hill, across the tracks, past the freight depot, to Dakota Avenue.

Georgie and Linnie bounced around so much trying to see everything that finally Mama took Linnie onto her lap. And Papa laid his hand on Georgie's shoulder, straightening her around so that she couldn't look out of the window, and so she missed seeing the turn onto Dakota Avenue. But she heard the wheels squeaking, so she knew that they had turned the corner.

When the car stopped at Pierre Street and Papa had helped them down the car step, Georgie was surprised to see a great many people walking around a platform where the streets crossed.

"Has that platform been here ever since Decoration Day?" she asked.

"Oh, no," Papa answered, "it was set up just for tonight."

"What is this show?" Mama asked. "Why are there so many Indians here?"

"You see," Papa explained, as he led them toward some chairs in the middle of the street, "our committee wants to entertain the people that come to look Pierre over. We want them to understand that this isn't a dangerous frontier town any more, and that the Indians are friendly. So we have hired a band of Sioux to give dances and races in the park and to camp there until election. This is a preview for Pierre citizens."

"Oh!" Mama exclaimed, "that sounds like a very bright idea."

As Georgie listened, she kept looking around for her friends. "I see Susan and the Brown girls across the street. But I don't see the twins. I should think they would be here to see the Indians."

"Mr. Smith sent them out to his brother's ranch for the summer," Papa told her.

"Oh!" Georgie thought. "I'd like to go to a ranch and ride real horses." Then she took a chair right in front of Papa.

An Indian woman in a full-gathered, blue calico dress and a plaid shawl edged into the crowd in front of Georgie. Hanging onto the woman's skirt was a girl about Georgie's size.

"She's as old as I am," Georgie thought, "and too big to act the way three-year-old Linnie does. I wonder what she is scared of."

With that the girl let loose of her mother's dress and turned around. She stared straight at Georgie out of her black eyes. Georgie stared back. When Georgie tried to make friends with her by smiling at her, the girl hid her face again in her mother's skirt.

Papa leaned over Georgie's shoulder to whisper, "That is Chief Red Feather's wife and his daughter in front of you."

"Oh!" Georgie said, as she watched the Indian woman squat down in the dust and pull the girl to lean against her.

The "tum-tum-tum" of a drum made Georgie look toward the platform. About a dozen Indian men were forming a circle around the drummer. She looked

with great interest at their beaded buckskin shirts and leggings and their beautiful feather war bonnets.

She leaned back to ask Papa, "Which one is Chief Red Feather?"

"The one with the finest headdress," Papa answered, "that bonnet of big white feathers that comes almost to his heels."

Georgie noticed that the chief was the first to move in time to the drums, stepping slowly and heavily, and then faster, as the drumming grew faster. In between looking at the dancers, Georgie glanced at the little girl.

As the drum sounded louder and the men stepped higher, the girl pulled away from her mother and stood up straight, clapping her hands softly in time to the music.

The dancers bent, straightened, and bent again, keeping their arms tightly folded against their bodies. Georgie felt her own feet keeping time to the drum.

When the Indians began to shout in time to the drum, the girl uttered a shout, too. But the mother pinched the girl's arm, and she crouched down again, hiding her face in her mother's big, blue skirt.

Georgie thought, "I guess little Indian girls have to learn to be ladies just the way white girls do."

When the drum stopped and the dancers left the platform, Georgie looked around for the Indian girl, but she couldn't see her anywhere.

"That's a good bunch of dancers," Papa remarked. "And there's a streetcar coming in right now. Let's go."

Georgie watched the driver as he stopped his mules, unhooked them from the front end of the car, drove them to the back and then hooked them up to that end.

"Why doesn't he turn the car around?" she asked.

"There is no room in the street for a big circle of track. This is the easy way to turn."

On the trip home Georgie asked, "Could I get acquainted with that Red Feather girl?"

"Well, I don't know," Papa answered. "You might try. Red Feather speaks English very well, but I rather think his family speaks only Dacotah. You might have to talk in sign language."

Chapter 14
Fourth of July

The morning following the Indian dance, Papa remarked, "In two weeks it will be the Fourth of July, and then the year will be half gone."

"I'm going to mark the days on a calendar until the Fourth," Georgie said, as she ran to a calendar hanging by Mama's desk.

"Here is a pencil," Linnie said. "Let me mark it." So Georgie showed her where to mark it. "We'll do this every day right after breakfast," she said.

On the morning that they marked July third, Georgie said, "This is the hottest day we have marked, and tomorrow, Linnie, is really and truly going to be the Fourth of July."

Linnie jumped up and down, clapping her hands. "Firecrackers!" she shouted.

Georgie saw Papa's eyes twinkle as he watched Linnie. "I'll bring the firecrackers home tonight," he promised.

That evening when the girls met Papa at the front door, Georgie was disappointed to see that he had nothing in his hands.

Linnie screamed, "Firecrackers! Where are the firecrackers, Papa?"

"Right here, baby," Papa replied, taking a flat package from his coat pocket.

"I'll look for the holders after dinner," he added, as he laid the package on the clock shelf.

"You put the holders in the box with your hammer," Georgie reminded him.

"That's right," Papa said, and he hunted up his tool box in the back shed. He put the holders that he had made from pieces of broomstick beside the firecrackers. "Now, no one must touch these until I can help you with them in the morning."

After dinner, Mama suggested, "Let's see if it is cooler on the front porch. It surely is a hot day." She took a palm-leaf fan from the table in the hall and gave one to Georgie. Then Mama sat in the porch rocker and fanned herself, while Georgie fanned Linnie as they sat on the top porch steps. Papa fastened the hose to the front hydrant and set it so that a spray of water blew across the steps.

Georgie enjoyed the cool spray. "I can hear firecrackers, but I can't see them," she called to Papa.

"Some young people in the next block are firing them in their back yards," he explained.

When Mama announced, "Bedtime, darlings!" Georgie complained, "I can't go to sleep when there is so much noise."

"Just lie down and shut your eyes," Papa told her, "and the next thing you know the cannon in the courthouse yard will go boom, and it will be morning."

Georgie shut her eyes as she lay quietly in bed, listening to the bang, bang, bang, sounding all over town. The next thing she knew there sounded a very big BOOM. She opened her eyes, and just as Papa had told her, it was morning! "Wake up!" she cried, shaking Linnie. "Wake up! It's the Fourth of July!"

Linnie bounced onto the floor and ran to the front bedroom, screaming, "Get up, Papa! It's Fourth of July!"

Georgie hurried into a dress and ran into the parlor, just as Papa came out of his bedroom, yawning.

"Linnie!" he exclaimed, "it's only five o'clock!"

"Please, Papa," Georgie begged, "let us fire our crackers!"

"All right," Papa agreed, but he was still yawning. "Let's get dressed and start celebrating. You help Linnie, Georgie."

Georgie dressed Linnie so fast that the girls beat Papa to the front porch. When he did come out, Georgie saw that he held the packages of crackers and the holders, and was blowing on the lighted end of a stick of punk. She watched carefully to see how he fitted a little "lady cracker" into a holder, gave it to Linnie, and then lighted the fuse.

"Point it at the gate," he told her.

"Fun!" Linnie shouted, as her cracker went off with a fizzy sort of noise. "Make me another, Papa!"

"Let me fix mine," Georgie begged. "I watched you. I know how."

"All right. It's going to take all my time to keep up with Linnie."

"I must do this very carefully, so that Papa will know that I am big enough to fire crackers by myself," Georgie murmured to herself.

"Watch out!" Papa called. "Your crackers are bigger than Linnie's."

Just at that moment Georgie's cracker went off with such a big bang that she dropped her holder. As she picked it up, she looked at Papa to see if he were going to help her next time, but he just smiled at her, so she fired another cracker without dropping the holder. "I guess Papa knows I'm a pretty big girl," she thought happily.

When Britta rang the breakfast bell, Georgie said, "There are only three left. Can't we fire them?"

Papa tied the three fuses together and laid them on the sidewalk. "Touch these off," he told Georgie, "and then run!"

Georgie reached as far as she could with the punk in her holder and touched the fuses with the lighted end. Then she made a dash for the porch. BANG BANGBANG!! "That was the most fun of all," she exclaimed, as they went into the house.

At the breakfast table Mama gave what Papa called, "The Orders of the Day."

"First, we will decorate the porch. Then you girls will play quietly in the yard with your dolls until we are ready to go to the park. After the parade and the speech in the park, we'll have our picnic dinner."

When breakfast was over, and after all the bunting and the flags had been draped on the front porch,

Georgie took Linnie out to the front gate to see how the house looked.

"It is just beautiful!" she called to Papa, who was standing on the top step mopping his face with his handkerchief. "I love flags! And I love Fourth of July!" Then she took Linnie's hand. "We'd better get Bessie and Helen Keller and go out to the swing," she said.

As she and Linnie played in the back yard, Georgie watched for Papa, who had gone to get Harry.

"There they are!" she cried at last. "Come, Linnie, let's get into the surrey."

"Georgie, you sit in front and help Mama drive, because I am going to ride in the parade. Linnie, you help Britta take care of the picnic basket in the back seat." Those were Papa's orders.

When everyone and everything was in place in the surrey, Papa gave Mama the reins and then he slid into the very end of the front seat, pushing Georgie to the middle. "The parade is forming," he said. "We must hurry!"

Mama slapped Harry with the reins, and off they went. When they stopped at Pierre Street and Papa had left them to join the parade, Mama said, "I'm glad people are riding in this parade. It's too hot to walk to the park." Just then the band began to play.

" 'Yankee Doodle!' " Georgie cried. "Listen, Linnie—'Yankee Doodle Goes to Town!' "

"There are the old soldiers and their wives," Mama interrupted.

"I see Papa!" Linnie shouted.

"He sees us," Georgie said, as she watched Papa. He was in a carriage with the rest of the Capital Committee, and as he spied his family, he raised his hat and waved it at them. Georgie waved back to him.

"Girls, look at the Indians!" Mama called.

Georgie looked carefully at the Indians riding on their spotted ponies. She thought she could tell which one was Red Feather, because of his long, white war bonnet.

"Firemen!" Linnie shouted.

After the firemen, who rode on their hook-and-ladder cart and their hose cart, fell into line, Mama said, "I think that is all. Maybe we can follow along now." She clucked to Harry and turned him into Pierre Street behind the firemen.

Georgie looked back, out of the surrey. "The Hamiltons are behind us, and there's a great, long line of carriages back of them," she said.

"Everyone in town goes to the Fourth of July doings in the park," Mama explained. "Now, don't talk to me any more. Harry is nervous because of all this noise. Slow, Harry! There, boy!"

Georgie stopped talking and listened to Harry go clop clop along the road to the park.

Papa met the carriage at the park gate. He led Harry to a tree, let down his checkrein so that he could eat grass, and then tied him.

Georgie saw the Hamiltons tying up their horse near by, so she ran to stand with Susan.

"You two girls take care of Linnie while we listen to the speech," Mama told them. Then the grown-ups walked over to join the crowd of people sitting in front of the speaker's table.

Georgie waved at them until she saw them take chairs right in front of the speaker. Then she turned to Susan. "What shall we do for fun?"

"Let's go to the river," Susan suggested.

Georgie took Linnie's hand and helped her through the long grass and out of the way of the rose-bushes, until they came to the riverbank.

"Oh, look! There are some Indian children wading," Susan exclaimed. "And they are shouting something."

"What are they saying?" Linnie asked.

"Papa says they talk Dacotah," Georgie answered, as she tried to pick out the Red Feather girl.

Linnie pulled at Georgie's hand. "I want to go back," she cried. "I want Mama!"

"All right," Georgie said. "Come, Susan!"

"Oh, Linnie!" she exclaimed, a moment later. "You walked right into that rosebush! Hold still, so you won't tear your dress."

"You've got to hold still!" Susan scolded, trying to help Georgie free Linnie.

"I want Mama!" Linnie screamed, as she tried to pull her dress away from the thorns herself.

Georgie laid Helen Keller on the ground. "Now stand still!" she ordered. "We can't help you when you pull so hard."

"Get me loose!" Linnie yelled. "They're coming! Hurry, Georgie!"

Georgie looked behind her and saw that the Indian children had come out of the water and were standing on the bank watching. She looked at the one nearest to her. "That's the chief's little girl, I think."

Then she saw the girl pick up Helen Keller. "That's my doll!" she cried. The Indian girl stood still, holding on to Helen Keller. Suddenly Georgie felt angry. "You can't have my doll!" she screamed, and snatched Helen Keller away from the girl. Then she ran for the surrey, with Susan and Linnie screaming behind her, "Wait for us, Georgie!"

When she reached the road, Georgie looked back. She saw that the Indian children had gone out of sight, and that Susan and Linnie were stumbling toward her in the long grass.

"I'm bleeding, Dodo!" Linnie was crying. "Help me, Dodo!" Georgie saw that Linnie's dress was torn and stained.

"I'm coming," she called. Then she put Helen Keller on the surrey seat, and went to meet Linnie.

"What made you run like that?" Susan asked, as the two girls wiped the blood from Linnie's fingers and the tears from her face.

"I thought that girl was going to steal Helen Keller," Georgie explained.

"I think she just wanted to look at her. She didn't run off with her—she just stood and held her."

"I didn't think of that," Georgie admitted. "Anyway, I'm not going to take my doll to picnics any more. She's safer at home."

"I don't want to go back to the river," Linnie sobbed.

"No, we'll play here," Georgie agreed. "We'll play house until the speech is over." She picked up Helen Keller from the seat of the surrey and held her very tight, glad that she still had her doll to play with.

Susan complained, "I don't want to play house. I'm hungry." She peeked in the Clark lunch basket. "Baked beans!" she cried. "M-m-m! I love baked beans!"

"Eggs!" said Linnie, who had climbed up into the surrey. Georgie suddenly felt hungry, too, so she gave Susan and Linnie each an egg and then took one for herself.

"I made the ham sandwiches all by myself," Susan boasted, leading the way to her surrey. She gave a sandwich to Georgie and one to Linnie, then took one for herself.

"Will your mama like our eating them now?" Georgie asked.

For answer, she heard her own mama's voice behind her. "Well, this mama doesn't like it very well that you couldn't wait until we could set out our picnic properly."

"Oh, well," Mrs. Hamilton admitted, coming up to Mama, "the speech was pretty long–I suppose they did get hungry."

As she helped spread the tablecloth on the grass and set out the food, Georgie felt that she really ought to explain about Linnie's scratches and torn dress, but when she saw Linnie sitting happily beside Britta and watching her cut watermelon, she decided to wait until she got home.

After Georgie had eaten so much that there wasn't room for one more bite, and after the two mamas and Britta began to pack things back into the baskets, Papa suggested, "Now, let's take in the races!"

"Where are they?" Georgie asked, as Papa headed Harry for the east gate of the park.

"First, the Indians are racing. Then there will be some races for boys and girls. Then the two fire companies will have a contest."

"May I race in the children's race?" Georgie asked. "I'm the fastest runner in school, except for Charles Smith."

"That's all right for you to race on the school grounds, but I wouldn't want my little lady to race in public," Mama said.

"Oh!" Georgie replied, thinking how very hard it was to grow up to be a lady.

When she saw the Indian racers, their bodies painted red, black, and white, and wearing bright feather headdresses, she began to wonder whether that little Indian girl would be there to watch her father. So that Hellen Keller would be safe, she put her under a fold of her gingham skirt and then placed her hand where she could feel the doll through the gingham.

"Which is Red Feather?" she asked. Sure enough, she had guessed right. Papa pointed at the figure with the long, trailing bonnet of white feathers.

"I guess the women and children are back in the park," Papa remarked, after looking around.

Then Georgie uncovered Helen Keller, but she continued to keep hold of her doll as it lay in her lap.

When the race began and the people shouted and yelled as they cheered on their favorite racers, Linnie began to cry. "I want to go home," she sobbed.

"Do you care a lot about these races?" Mama asked Papa. "Linnie seems very tired, and she's gotten all scratched up from running in the park. Let's go home."

"All right," Papa agreed. "We'll go home. It has been a long day."

All during the drive home, Georgie held Helen Keller tightly. When Mama was putting Linnie to bed, Georgie took her doll into the under-the-porch house. "Helen Keller," she told her, "you must stay away from that Red Feather girl. She is likely to steal you." Then she looked at her doll, who was sitting up very straight against an apple crate. "I pulled you away awfully fast," she admitted. "I could have let her hold you until we got Linnie loose from the rosebush. Maybe Susan is right—maybe she just wanted to hold you.

Do you think if I went back to the park and let that girl hold you a little while, it would make her happy?"

Helen Keller looked at Georgie out of her clear, blue eyes and did not answer.

It was too hot under the porch to stay very long, so Georgie took her doll to the swing, where it was cool and shady. They swung a long time, smelling the hot summer smells of cut grass and of sweet clover, and watching little green grasshoppers jump from one weed to another. They swung until Mama called them in for supper.

Chapter 15
A Personal Contribution

After the Fourth of July celebration was past, Georgie thought a great deal about the Indian girl. When she was swinging with Helen Keller, she thought about how Charles had swung out on that grapevine, and she wondered whether the Indian girl used a grapevine for a swing. "I think maybe it would be fun to play with that girl," she told Helen Keller.

Whenever anyone mentioned the Indians in the park, Georgie listened to hear whether anything would be said about the little Red Feather girl. But she didn't even hear Red Feather's name mentioned until one hot evening late in July.

As the family sat on the front porch, fanning themselves with palm-leaf fans, Georgie heard Papa say, "Mac, our interpreter, was in the office today. He told us that the Indian women in the park want to go home because they don't have enough work to do."

"Why don't they make beaded moccasins to sell to the visitors?" Mama suggested.

"That's a real good idea," Papa replied.

"What's an interpreter?" Georgie asked, remembering what her papa had said.

"He's someone who understands two or more languages," Papa answered. "Mac understands both English and Dacotah, so he can help us to understand the Indians."

"Could he help Red Feather's little girl understand me?"

"I suppose so, if he had the time," Papa answered, "but he's a busy man."

The very next noon Papa said to Georgie, "Mama wants to take a nap with Linnie, and I told her you could ride along with me."

"I'd love that," Georgie answered, picking up Helen Keller from her rocking chair, "as soon as I put my doll away."

"Oh, bring it with you! I'm in a hurry."

Georgie ran after him with Helen Keller in her arms and climbed over the wheel into the buggy. "Where are we going?" she inquired.

"Down to the park to talk with Red Feather. I told Mac I'd be there at one o'clock, and it's five minutes to one right now." He clucked to Harry to make him go faster.

Georgie held Helen Keller a little tighter, as she asked, "Do you think Red Feather's girl would like to play with me?"

"I don't know," Papa answered. "She's probably rather bashful. There's Mac now!"

A rider, who wore a big felt hat and leather chaps, came up even with the buggy. "Howdy, Clark," he greeted Georgie's papa.

"Hello, Mac! What do you think of our committee buying skins and beads for these women to make into souvenirs for Pierre visitors?"

"Good idea," Mac replied.

"Now that the harvest is over," Papa went on, "there will be a great many more visitors coming here. We've got to keep the Indians to entertain them."

"Anything I can do, just whistle for me," Mac agreed, riding alongside the buggy.

When he reached the park, Papa drove up to the largest tepee, where Red Feather and his wife were standing. Georgie watched Mac as he jumped off his horse and dropped the reins to the ground. She listened to what Red Feather said, but of course she could not understand the words. When Mac began to answer him in Dacotah, Georgie noticed a little girl come out of the tepee and pull on her mother's skirt.

Then she felt Papa's hand on her knee. "Georgie," he said, "try to play with that little girl. She's bothering her mother, and I'm in a hurry to finish this business and get back to the office."

Georgie held Helen Keller carefully as she jumped over the wheel of the buggy to the ground. Then she walked toward the girl, but she hurried around to the other side of her mother.

"I just want to play with you," Georgie began, holding out Helen Keller toward her.

The girl peeked around her mother's skirt, so Georgie moved closer. "This is Helen Keller," she said. "Don't you want to hold her?"

Then Georgie remembered that the little girl did not understand English, so she stopped talking, but moved closer to the girl. When she came very close, the girl stepped away from her mother and reached for Helen Keller. Georgie put the doll into the girl's brown hand, watching to see if it made her happy. The girl hugged the doll. Then she ran into the tepee, holding her cheek close to Helen Keller's china face as she ran.

Georgie waited, hoping that Red Feather's little girl would bring the doll back so that they could play with it together, but the girl did not come back.

Then Georgie heard Papa say, "That's fine, Mac! Tell them to charge the leather and the beads to me. Are you ready, Georgie?"

Georgie saw that Papa was reaching for Harry's reins, but she turned back quickly to look at the tepee. She had just meant to lend Helen Keller to the Indian girl for a few minutes. She felt tears stinging her eyes.

"Come, Georgie!" Papa called. So she climbed slowly into the buggy and sat down. Papa clucked to Harry. At that moment Georgie saw Mrs. Red Feather talking to Mac, and Mac reaching for Harry's bridle. She heard him say, "Just a minute, Clark! She says her girl has your girl's doll. She'll make her give it back."

Georgie remembered the happy look on the little girl's face as she put her cheek against Helen Keller's, and she thought, "That girl really loves Helen Keller."

"I'll give her Helen Keller," she decided shakily.

"You're sure you want to do that?"

"Won't it help Pierre to get the capital if the Red Feather girl is happy?"

"Well, yes—anything that keeps the Indians willing to stay here until election would help," Papa answered.

"Then it's all right," Georgie whispered.

"Georgie gave her the doll," Papa called to Mac. "Tell them it is all right."

When Georgie arrived home without Helen Keller, Mama asked, "Why did you do it, dear?" as she put her arms around Georgie and hugged her.

Georgie sobbed, "She wanted her."

"But Papa could have bought her a doll. You did not have to give her your very own Helen Keller, darling."

"She wanted Helen Keller," Georgie repeated, leaning against Mama's shoulder and letting a few tears roll down her cheeks. "And I wanted to help Papa get the capital."

"Well, there are other ways to help Papa. And he can drive right downtown and buy a store doll for that child this very afternoon. We'll get Helen Keller back, Georgie."

Georgie shook her head. She understood that the little girl might love Helen Keller and might not love any other doll, but she didn't know how to explain that to Mama.

"No!" she cried, "I *gave* Helen Keller to her."

"Tush! Such a lot of talk about a doll!" Papa said. "Let Georgie do it if she wants to. Red Feather will brag about his girl and my girl being friends. Georgie did all right!"

Georgie reached for Mama's handkerchief and wiped her eyes with it. When she later gathered up

Helen Keller's dresses to give them to Linnie, she said, "It's a good thing that the two dolls are the same size."

"When you put Helen Keller's dresses on Bessie, you can play that she really is Helen Keller," Linnie said.

"I'm too old for dolls. You can have Bessie all for yourself."

After she picked up the doll dress that she had made out of the brown and white percale pieces left from her own dress, she decided to put on her own secretary dress and write a report for Papa. When she finished it, she put it beside his dinner plate.

Pierre, South Dakota
July 31, 1890

Report
I gave my Helen Keller to Red Feather's little girl to help Pierre get the capital.
G. Clark, Sec.

After Papa read it, Georgie peeked over his arm to see what he would write on the edge this time. "Personal Contribution," he wrote, and aloud, he said, "If all the voters made such valuable contributions, we'd surely win the campaign."

That night, after her regular prayers, and when Mama had gone out to the front porch to sit with Papa in the moonlight, Georgie had another talk with God.

"Dear God," she prayed, "when I asked you to let me help Papa get the capital, I didn't mean that I should have to give away Helen Keller. But please let Helen Keller help us to get the capital. And please, dear God, help that little Indian girl to take good care of Helen Keller."

Then she went to sleep, feeling away down in her bones that now surely Pierre would get to keep the capital.

Chapter 16

Real Secretary Work

At breakfast the morning after Georgie had given Helen Keller away, Mama said, "Georgie, your birthday is coming soon. Why don't you and Linnie mark off the days as you did for Fourth of July?"

Georgie walked slowly over to the calendar and counted the days until August twenty-third. Then she marked out August first. "It is a pretty long time," she said. Somehow she didn't feel very much interested now that she could not share her birthday with Helen Keller.

After breakfast, Linnie suggested, "Let's play house with Bessie under the porch."

Georgie nodded and followed Linnie to their playroom.

"Why don't you talk?" Linnie asked.

"I'm lonesome for Helen Keller," Georgie confessed.

"Mama said Papa could get her back."

"Then the Indian girl would be lonesome for her. I guess I can stand it better than she can."

After Georgie had watched Linnie change Bessie's clothes, she suggested, "Let's go to Susan's."

"All right, Dodo." Linnie placed Bessie on the orange crate and took Georgie's hand.

Georgie understood that Linnie was trying to comfort her. She squeezed Linnie's hand all the way to the front yard, where they found Mama weeding her flower bed.

"Be home by eleven," Mama warned them. "I may need you to help me then."

Linnie danced and skipped all the way to the Hamilton gate, but Georgie walked slowly, wondering how to tell Susan about Helen Keller.

When they reached Susan's house, the first thing Susan suggested was "Let's play dolls."

"We didn't bring ours," Georgie replied, feeling her cheeks grow hot. "Let's play hoops."

"Georgie gave away Helen Keller," Linnie exclaimed.

"Gave her away!" Susan gasped. "Georgie, you couldn't! Who'd you give her to?"

"To Red Feather's girl." Georgie tried to sound as if she didn't care very much. "Papa said it was a personal contribution to the campaign," she added. Then she picked up a hoop and rolled it down the sidewalk to her own gate.

By the time she had rolled it back to Susan's gate, Susan and Linnie were racing their hoops, so she didn't have to talk any more for a while.

When Susan tired of rolling hoops, she threw herself on the grass, shouting, "Let's rest a while."

"We've got to go home," Georgie said, afraid Susan would begin to talk about Helen Keller; so she took Linnie's hand and dragged her through the gate. "Good-by, Susan," she called over her shoulder, "I had a good time."

"It isn't eleven! I want to stay!" Linnie argued.

"I don't want to play with Susan any more today. I'll play anything you want if you won't cry about going home so soon," Georgie promised.

"Mudpies?" Linnie asked eagerly.

"All right," Georgie agreed. So they played mudpies until Mama called them to come indoors to lunch.

After lunch, and while Linnie was napping, Georgie sat in the swing and wondered whether Red Feather's girl was swinging on a grapevine with Helen Keller, or whether maybe she had taken the doll into the river and had got Helen Keller's cloth body wet.

That idea worried Georgie so much that she felt she just had to go down to the park to find out how Helen Keller was. She knew Mama would not give her permission to go, but at that minute it seemed more important to look after her doll than to mind Mama. So Georgie jammed her hat onto her head and hurried out the front gate.

She walked to the courthouse and stood on the steps, looking down Pierre Street.

As she stood she thought, "I'd have to go away beyond Papa's office, then turn onto Dakota Avenue and walk ever so far to get to the park. Probably someone who knows Papa would see me and would ask if that wasn't George Clark's girl, and would take me to Papa. Maybe Papa would spank me for running away."

So she went home and looked again at the calendar. "It's three weeks until my birthday," she said to herself, "and nothing to do all that time!"

Morning after morning, Georgie marked off the days on the calendar. At last she came to the week of her birthday. As she marked off August twenty-one,

Mama asked, "Would it be a big enough party if I would just ask Susan and the Brown girls? There is so much to do before election that I'm afraid I won't have time to plan a big party."

"That's all right," Georgie answered. "You don't need to give me any party at all, if that will help to get the capital," but inside, she was glad she could have even a small party.

Two mornings later, before they were even dressed, Georgie hurried Linnie to the calendar. "I'm going to mark August twenty-three in red," she said, "because it is my birthday today."

While she was crossing out the "23" with a red pencil, she felt herself being lifted into the air. "Oh, Papa!" she screamed, "I'm too big to be tossed! I'm ten now!"

"Ten spanks and one to grow on, then," Papa laughed, giving her ten little spanks and a great, big one that sent her forward toward Mama, who stood watching them.

Then Georgie felt Mama's warm arms around her. "Ten kisses for my birthday girl!" Mama exclaimed.

"Me, too!" Linnie kept screaming, so Georgie bent down and let Linnie kiss her ten times.

When she and Linnie had finished dressing and had come to the breakfast table, Britta carried in a big platter of pancakes and set it in front of Georgie. "Happy birthday!" she said.

"This is a real special breakfast," Georgie remarked happily as she covered her pancakes with butter and maple syrup. "It's fun to be ten!"

"Now this is a surprise day for Georgie," Mama said, as they left the breakfast table, "so you girls stay out of the house until lunchtime."

"I'll take care of Georgie," Linnie promised importantly. "We'll find something to do."

After lunch, Mama told Georgie, "I'm going to be busy in the kitchen for a while. You may dress yourself while Linnie naps. The girls will be here at two o'clock."

"Yes, Mama," Georgie answered. "Come, Linnie, I'll help you take your nap."

After Linnie was asleep, and while she was putting on her best white dress and tying her pretty pink sash, Georgie began to hunt. She hunted in all the bureau drawers and behind Mama's desk, but she couldn't find any packages.

"I wish I knew what I will get," she thought, as she dug into a dark corner behind some boxes in the closet. "I hope it won't be a doll. I don't want a doll if I can't have Helen Keller."

After Linnie had waked up, Georgie barely had time to button her sister into her Sunday dress before the doorbell rang.

"Come in," she called to Susan and Erma and Amy as she opened the door.

"Happy birthday!" they all shouted and chased her around the parlor, trying to spank her ten times.

As Georgie ran away from them, she bumped into Mama, who was coming from the kitchen. "Oh, Mama!" she screamed, "save me!" When they saw Mama, the girls stopped their chasing and stood still.

"We'll have the presents first," Mama began, "if you will all sit down. Then we'll have the refreshments."

They did sit down, as Mama requested, and then Susan rose and walked over to Georgie, handing her a sewing box. "It has a real embroidery hoop in it," she said, "and needles and thimbles and scissors."

"Thank you very much." Georgie wished Susan had remembered that she didn't have a doll to sew for any more.

When she had put Erma's string of beads around her neck and had tied Amy's pink ribbons, instead of her old white ones, on the ends of her braids, she twirled around twice to show them off. "Thank you very much," she said to Amy and to Erma. "See how nicely the ribbons and the beads match my sash!"

Linnie gave her a funny piece of blue velvet that had been gathered together by long stitches. "It is a purse for you to put your money into," she explained.

Georgie knew that Linnie liked to be praised, so she kissed her as she said, "It is very beautiful. You sewed it very nicely. Thank you, Linnie."

Then Mama went into the front bedroom. Georgie thought, "It's probably a book." When Mama came back, pushing something ahead of her, Georgie screamed, "A desk! A real desk!"

"This is from Papa," Mama said. "Look inside."

Georgie looked admiringly at the desk, which was almost exactly like her school desk. It had a slanting lid that could be lifted up, so that books could be stored in the box underneath. In the box was a note. "Birthday greetings to a very good secretary, from Papa," it said.

"What does that mean?" Amy asked.

"I did some secretary work for Papa," Georgie explained, feeling very much more grownup than Amy.

Then Mama brought in a cardboard box, which she set on the desk. "It looks like a doll box," Georgie thought, "and I don't want a doll!"

As soon as she took the cover off the box she gasped. There lay a great big doll with its eyes closed in its beautifully painted bisque face. It had real hair, brown, just like Georgie's. It was the most beautiful doll she had ever dreamed of owning.

"Oh!" she cried. "Oh, Mama! How gorgeous! Thank you, Mama!"

Lying beside the doll was a large square, thick envelope. As Georgie opened it, she could see that it was full of patterns, just like the ones Mama used—really, truly patterns!

Susan reached for the patterns. "Goody, goody!" she cried. "Now we can make our doll dresses right, instead of guessing at them. What fun we will have, Georgie!"

"Using these patterns will help you be a good dressmaker, Georgie. I think you are old enough to learn how to make your own dresses soon."

Suddenly Georgie felt very much grownup. She had a real desk, a real workbox, and real patterns, together with a doll that the patterns would fit. She hugged Mama very tight as she said, "Thank you."

When she heard the girls shout, "How pretty!" she turned from Mama to see Britta standing in the kitchen doorway and holding a big cake blazing with candles.

"You girls can sit at the table," Mama said, "and watch Georgie cut her cake while Britta serves the ice cream."

"You must make a wish, first," Erma told her. So Georgie shut her eyes and wished; then she blew hard.

"You blew them all out!" Amy cried. "You'll get your wish—what was it, Georgie?"

"For Pierre to get the capital," Georgie exclaimed.

"Now we know that Pierre will win," Susan said, as they all clapped their hands.

After the cake and the ice cream had been eaten, Susan suggested a game. "Let's play 'office.' Georgie, you be the boss and sit at your desk and tell us what to do."

They played "office" until Mama brought the girls' hats and told them, "Your mothers will be expecting you home."

"We've had a lovely time," the girls said to Georgie as they went out the front door. She waved good-by to them until they had gone through the gate, then she shut the door and went to find Mama. "I've had a wonderful birthday, Mama," she said, as she hugged her.

When Papa come home, Georgie showed him her presents.

"This is Viola," she said, holding the new doll for him to see. "I can't ever love another doll as much as I did Helen Keller, but I think it will be easier to sew for Viola. I just love my desk, Papa. Can I do some secretary work for you?"

"The office girls sometimes don't have time to finish the letters, and I have to do it. The next time that happens, I might bring you some envelopes to put the stamps on."

"I'd like that," Georgie answered. "I'd put the stamps on real square."

"I hope there won't be so much office work that we can't get our sewing done—school starts in a week," Mama reminded them.

"I can do my secretary work at night and my dressmaking in the daytime," Georgie offered, adding, "it would go a lot faster to sew Viola's dresses on the sewing machine—could I, please?"

"Wel-l-l," Mama answered slowly, "you'll have to learn how some day. Perhaps this is as good a time as any."

"Oh, goody!" Georgie exclaimed, finding it hard to keep still, as her feet seemed to want to dance because she was so happy. "When can I start?"

"Tomorrow morning, I guess," Mama replied.

The following Saturday Georgie showed Papa two dresses she had sewed for Viola on the machine. "I think I can begin to sew my own dresses soon," she told him.

She saw Papa's eyes twinkle as he asked Mama, "How about that?"

"You have done very well," Mama approved, "but you have some more to learn before you are able to make a whole dress for yourself. I think you have learned enough so that you can be a real help when Mrs. Larson comes to do the fall sewing after Election Day."

"I can hardly wait to show Mrs. Larson Viola's dresses," Georgie said, remembering that last spring all she had been able to do to help was to keep Linnie out of Mrs. Larson's way. Now Linnie was big enough to play by herself, and Georgie was big enough to sew on the machine.

The next Monday morning at school, Georgie felt tall as she walked past Miss May's room to the fifth-sixth-grade room. "I'm a fifth-grader now!" she thought happily.

When she was assigned a seat, she found that the Smith twins were seated across the aisle from her.

"Did you have a good time at the ranch?" she asked them.

"I can ride a calf!" Charles bragged.

"I can rope a calf, almost alone," Richard added.

Then the big bell stopped ringing, and the teacher rapped on her desk for the class to come to order .

On the way home after school, Richard said, "We have a campaign job. We are going to hand out VOTE-FOR-PIERRE cards to the visitors as they get on the evening train."

"I have a job, too," Georgie said, proudly. "I am a secretary!"

"Can I help sometimes?" Susan asked. "I'd like to be a secretary, too."

"Probably on Saturdays you could be my assistant secretary," Georgie answered.

That very evening Papa brought home some letters for Georgie to work on. He ruled a sheet of paper for her on which to keep records. "Turn it in at the end of the campaign," he told her.

Georgie put on her secretary dress and went right to work. When Mama told her it was bedtime, Georgie wrote on her record sheet: "September 1, 1890. I sealed and stamped 10 letters."

As she undressed, she told Mama, "I just love being a secretary."

The next morning Linnie asked, "Why don't we mark days, any more?"

Mama suggested, "You could mark the days until Election Day. That will be the second Tuesday in November, the eleventh."

"I want to," Linnie said.

"Wait," Georgie said quickly. "You can mark, but I will tell you where to mark. See, Linnie, here is today. Cross it out. My! what a lot of days for me to do secretary work!"

Finally the morning arrived when Papa said, as he picked up a pile of stamped envelopes, "That's the last of this work! It's so near election that there is not time to mail out anything more. We're paying off our help tonight."

Georgie looked at the calendar. "Here, Linnie," she called, "we just have today and tomorrow and Monday to mark. Then it's election." The thought that the capital would be decided in three days made her feel creepy.

"You'd better give me your final report now," Papa told her, "if you have it made out."

Georgie hurried to her desk and added up all her records. Then she wrote:

Pierre, South Dakota
November 8, 1890

Final Report
I put 450 letters in envelopes. I sealed and stamped 630 letters. I worked 53 days. Susan helped me four days.

G. Clark, Sec.

When she gave the report to Papa, he said, "I'll attend to it soon."

"I think that means he will pay me real money," Georgie told Linnie.

"Then you can put it in the purse I made for your birthday," Linnie said.

When Papa came home that evening, he gave Georgie a large brown envelope. When Georgie reached her hand in, she uttered a little squeal as she drew out the pen and the inkstand that she had seen on Papa's desk at headquarters.

"We gave our pens to the office girls for souvenirs," Papa explained. He added, "There's a little envelope in there, too."

When Georgie drew out the small envelope, a bright coin fell out. Georgie thought it was a penny, and was so disappointed to receive so little for so much work that she let Linnie pick it up while she read the letter:

> Pierre, South Dakota
> November 8, 1890
>
> To a faithful secretary with thanks and appreciation from the Capital Committee.
>
> George Clark, Chairman

"Here, Linnie!" Papa cried. "Don't throw that money around that way! It's Georgie's salary."

Georgie was surprised that he should care what Linnie did with a penny. "She can have it," Georgie thought. "I wasn't really working for money, anyway —I was working for the capital."

Then Mama spoke. "Linnie, dear, give Georgie her five-dollar gold piece."

"Five-dollar gold piece!" Georgie screamed, taking the coin from Linnie and looking at it carefully. It was a five-dollar gold piece!

"Oh, Papa!" she cried, running to hug him, "that's grownup money!"

"You did a good job, Georgie," he said, patting her shoulder. "It was worth that much at least."

Georgie took the beautiful coin to her desk.

"Put it in my purse," Linnie begged. So Georgie tucked it carefully into the velvet purse and laid it in the box part of her desk.

When she looked up after closing the desk, she saw that Mama was helping Papa on with his coat in the front hall and that they were talking in low voices.

"I think Papa and Mama are worried about the election," she remarked to Linnie. "And I am, too. Even having all this money wouldn't be any good if Pierre lost the capital."

"Pierre will win," Linnie promised. "Don't you remember, Georgie? You blew out all your candles!"

"I hope so," Georgie answered. "We'll know for sure next Tuesday."

Chapter 17
The Election

At their Sunday breakfast, Mama said, "Papa is so worn out that he didn't sleep well last night. Let's be very quiet this morning so as not to wake him. We'll go to church by ourselves."

On the way to church, Georgie remarked, "It seems queer to go to church without Papa."

"I think the Lord understands how tired he is," Mama explained.

When they came home from Sunday School, Georgie was glad to see that Papa was dressed and lying on the sofa in the parlor.

"Do you feel better?" she asked, as she walked up close to him.

"My head aches to split," he replied. "Please tell Mama that Britta has given me toast and coffee, so I won't be eating any dinner."

When Georgie gave the message to Mama, she said, "Please ask Britta if she'd mind setting the dinner out in the kitchen today, since Papa isn't coming to the table."

When Georgie went to give the message to Britta, she found that Britta already had the sitting-room table set. "You can help put these things in the kitchen, Georgie," Britta said. "That poor man! He don't want noise and talking."

"This is a funny day," Georgie remarked, as she passed her plate for a second helping of pork roast and gravy, "it doesn't really seem like Sunday."

"It's a day in a lifetime," Mama explained, "and I want you girls to be helpers by keeping real still all afternoon. How about playing under the porch?"

Georgie no longer liked to play under the porch. She told herself the reason was that she was too old to play house, but she knew in her heart it was because "her own house" didn't seem right without Helen Keller. Then she thought about Papa lying on the sofa, a wet towel on his head to stop his headache, so she said,

"Do you want to make some mudpies, Linnie, and frost them pink with brick dust?"

"Oh, yes!" Linnie answered. "I love mudpies and cakes, Dodo." So they played under the porch all afternoon.

Because it was Britta's day to visit with other Norwegian girls who worked in Pierre, Georgie and Linnie helped Mama to set out the Sunday evening supper.

Papa came to the table. "Thank you, girls," he said, "for keeping so quiet."

"Can I yell now?" Linnie asked.

"Hush!" Mama cautioned her. "Ladies don't yell."

"Then can I play with Viola?"

"If you're real careful," Georgie told her.

"Then we'll play dolls in the bedroom," Linnie said, "and I won't yell." They played dolls until Mama told them it was time for bed. For once, Georgie was glad of bedtime. "It has been an awfully pokey sort of day," she said to Mama.

"Well, you have been a good helper."

As Georgie was putting on her coat the following morning, she heard Mama ask Papa, "Why don't you stay at home today, too? There's nothing to do but wait."

"I lay around all day yesterday. I think I'd better go to the office today—there are some odds and ends to be attended to."

Georgie thought she'd rather help Papa at the office than go to school, but nothing ever stopped school!

At noon, she was surprised to find a young man standing in the kitchen, watching Mama and Britta as they packed a lunch basket.

"Do you suppose that is enough?" Mama asked the young man.

"I don't believe they are very hungry," he replied. "They are the nervousest men I ever see—all they do is talk about what the odds are for Pierre."

When the man had taken the basket and had gone out to his buggy, Georgie asked Mama, "What are odds?"

"The chances of Pierre's winning," Mama replied.

At dinner that evening, Georgie noticed that Papa had eaten only a very little before he folded his napkin and asked Mama if he might be excused. Georgie wondered whether Britta felt hurt, for this meal was one of Britta's extra special dinners: chicken dumplings and gelatin salad and chocolate pudding. Georgie even ate a little more than she really wanted, to show Britta that she appreciated her efforts.

Papa read the *Pierre Daily Capital-Journal* while the family finished eating. Then he said to Mama, "I guess I'll get a shave. Probably the boys at the barber shop will have all the latest news. Don't sit up for me. Maybe some of us will try to get news at the telegraph office in the depot. I may be very late."

Georgie thought Mama was pretty nervous too, because of the way she hurried her and Linnie into bed earlier than usual. She tried to stay awake until Papa came home, but the next thing she knew Britta was shaking her gently, and it was morning.

"Your papa and mama are asleep. Linnie, too—you dress real still and come to the kitchen to eat."

So Georgie had to start off to school without saying good-by to anyone but Britta.

At school everything seemed just as usual. It hardly seemed possible that today the capital question was being decided by people voting all over South Dakota.

When Georgie came home to lunch, Linnie opened the door and shouted, "Mama is driving voters!"

Georgie was puzzled, and she asked Britta, "What does she mean?"

"That one!" Britta answered. "I don't know. Your mama will be home to dinner tonight, and then we'll know."

Georgie bolted her food and ran out to meet Susan. As they walked back to school, Susan explained, "My mama and your mama are going to drive all day, taking people to vote."

"Is your papa nervous?" Georgie asked.

"Awfully nervous," Susan replied. "I guess everyone in Pierre is. Oh, Georgie, I hope we win!"

"I do, too. I hope it more than anything!"

When Mama came home, Britta already had dinner on the table. Mama threw her cape over a chair, as she said, "Let's make this a fast meal. Papa is sending a buggy to take me back to the office. Georgie, I'm depending on you to put Linnie to bed."

Georgie saw Linnie's face pucker up, but she thought maybe it was best not to pay any attention to her sister. "Did you vote?" she asked Mama.

Mama laid down her knife and fork and looked soberly at Georgie. "Only men vote, Georgie. Women and criminals, insane people, and Indians aren't supposed to know enough to vote."

Georgie felt that rule wasn't fair at all. "I think you know enough!" she said.

"I think so, too," Mama laughed. "Anyway, Mrs. Hamilton and I saw to it that a lot of lazy men voted today."

After dinner, Linnie came close to Mama and begged, "You put me to bed, please, Mama."

"You let Georgie do it," Mama answered, patting her little girl's face. "The Western Union is going to get reports by wire from each town as the voting is over, and they will send the reports to the office. I want to be there with Papa when the reports come in."

Mama threw her cape over her shoulders. "I hear the buggy now," she called. "Good-by, darlings!"

"Mama!" Linnie screamed.

Mama looked at Georgie. "You know how to manage her," she said. "You can do it." Then she ran out to the buggy.

Georgie felt that Mama had spoken to her almost as if she were grownup. She put her arms around Linnie.

"Come, Linnie," she said, "I'll let you hold Viola." She took her handkerchief from her pocket and made Linnie blow her nose and wipe her eyes.

"I want Mama," Linnie still sobbed, as she leaned on Georgie.

Georgie understood how it scared Linnie to see Papa and Mama look so worried. It scared her, too, but she found Viola and put her in Linnie's arms.

"Mama has to take care of Papa," she explained, "and I will take care of you, and you will take care of Viola, and Viola will take care of Bessie. Won't that be nice?"

When they were both ready for bed, Georgie said, "Our poor dollies are so sleepy that they are being bad girls tonight. They won't go to sleep unless we lie down with them."

Linnie giggled. "We'd better spank them."

"No, I think we'd better sing them to sleep, and then when they are fast asleep, we can get up and put on our robes and wait for Mama," Georgie suggested.

That idea pleased Linnie very much. "But I'm going to get up and wait for Mama," she said, "just as soon as Viola and Bessie go to sleep."

When Georgie had sung all the lullabies she knew, she peeked at Linnie. "She's fast asleep," she thought. "I would like to get up and wait for Papa and Mama, but I guess they wouldn't like that very well, so I'll just lie still and listen for them."

She heard the mantel clock strike eight, then the half-hour—and the next thing she knew the clock was striking four and someone was opening the front door.

She slipped out of bed and ran into Mama's arms. "Who got the capital?" she cried anxiously.

"We did!" Papa exclaimed, joyfully.

At that moment a terrible roar shook the windows so hard that Georgie jumped.

"The cannon!" Mama exclaimed.

"The town is crazy," Papa added, "firing guns like Fourth of July!"

Georgie caught a glimpse of a rosy glow through the front windows.

"It's a bonfire!" Mama cried. "Oh, George, let's go to see it!"

"Do you want to go with us?" Papa asked Georgie.

"Oh, yes! I do! Wait for me!"

Mama helped her into her clothes so fast that the legs of her union suit made big bumps under her stockings.

"But who cares!" Mama whispered. "And let's not wake Linnie. She is too little to go with us."

Papa helped Georgie into her coat, and they all ran out into the cold night air. As they ran, Georgie saw a bonfire flare up in the street in front of the courthouse. The people who were running and jumping around it looked like black shadows against its blaze.

She heard a man shout through a horn, "Hurrah for Pierre for the capital!" When they got up close to the fire, someone started to sing, "Peerless Pierre."

Georgie was glad that Miss May had taught them that song in school, and she joined in, singing as loudly as she could.

She saw Charles and Richard helping the young men to pile boxes and branches on the fire. She felt the heat burning her, so she opened her coat and stepped back several feet from the fire. As she did so, Susan came up behind her and hugged her.

By that time the grownups were marching around the fire. "Let's march, too," Susan suggested.

Then she heard the bells—first the fire bell, then the school bell, then the church bell across the street.

"Oh, Susan! Isn't this fun?" she cried.

"Somebody's shooting!" Susan screamed.

Mama came up beside them. "It will be a mercy if no one is shot!" she cried, and then stepped back into the line that was circling the fire. Georgie thought she had never seen Mama act so much like a little girl.

Papa was different, too. He was slapping men on the back and shouting, "We did it! We licked them!"

Everyone seemed to be different, and everybody acted so excited.

"I've never had so much fun!" Georgie gasped, as Susan dragged her faster and faster around the fire.

At last she heard Papa say in his usual calm voice, "The sun is coming up. We must get this child home!"

"I don't want to go!" Georgie cried.

"It's about over," Papa said, taking one of her hands, while Mama took the other one.

"Let's run!" Papa said. They ran so fast that they almost dragged Georgie, although she worked her legs fast to keep up.

When they reached the front door, Papa opened it with a low bow. "Enter the home of the next attorney general."

Georgie burst past him into the sitting room and screamed, "Wake up, Linnie! Papa is elected, and Pierre is the capital. Linnie, wake up! We won!"

Chapter 18
Expressions Used in Georgie's Day

Baseburner: A stove or furnace used to heat a room. It stood up rather tall, was either cylindrical or square, had a hopper which could be reached by opening the top, and which held coal to feed the fire below. It had a door or doors in front through which to put kindling to start a fire, or to poke the fire. Usually there was an ornamental metal bar or shelf on the lower part on which a person could rest his feet.

Bustle: A pad worn under the back of a woman's skirt, and fastened at the waistline, to show the full drape of a dress.

Butter plate: A flat dish, usually of china, about three inches in diameter, used to hold an individual serving of butter.

Canton flannel: A heavy twilled cotton material with a fluffy back, often used for nightclothes.

Carpet beater: An implement shaped like a tennis racket, but slightly larger, made of loosely woven rattan or of leather strips, and used to beat the dust out of a carpet or rug thrown over a clothesline.

China silk: Originally, silk imported from China. In 1890 the name was used for any soft, thin, plain-weave silk.

Cookstove: An iron stove with a flat top made of round "griddles" and an iron framework into which they fitted. The firebox was at the left end, and could be filled with coal by taking off a griddle, or could be filled with wood by opening a door at top front of firebox. Below this door was the shaker; below that the ash door through which the ashpan could be removed. The left end of the stove had an opening by which the draft could be regulated. The oven took up most of the front. All stoves had connection with the outside air by means of a stovepipe running up through the roof into a brick chimney. The cookstove was simpler and cheaper than the iron or steel "range," which by 1890 had become standard equipment in large cities.

Derby: A man's hat made of stiff, hard felt. It had a melon-shaped crown and a rather narrow brim.

Guimpe: A high-necked, long-sleeved blouse worn under a jumper, and usually buttoned in the back.

Hitching post: Usually in Pierre in 1890, a six-by-six square, wooden post, about three feet high, and furnished with an iron ring through which the reins of a saddle horse or the hitching strap of a carriage horse could be tied. The post was set far enough into the road so that the horse could not paw the wooden sidewalk.

Horse block: A block of wood, concrete, or stone about 24 by 36 inches, the top of which was about 12 inches from the ground. It was set at a convenient distance from the hitching post to enable a lady to step gracefully from the horse block to a small iron step hanging from the floor of the buggy, and then into the buggy.

Horse (or mule) car: A streetcar seating about a dozen people, running on rails, and drawn by one or more horses, or mules. In Pierre mules were used because they were strong enough to pull a car carrying a full load up a steep grade. Rails were necessary because the unpaved streets were often so deep with mud or snow that even a team of mules could not pull a car without the help of well-cleared rails.

Ingrain carpet: A carpet made of yard-wide strips of "ingrain carpeting" sewed together by hand. It was woven of yarn "dyed in the grain" before weaving, so that both sides of the carpet were usable. It was considered "common," and used by people who did not have much money.

Pasqueflower: The state flower of South Dakota.

Prince Albert coat: A long frock coat, with a double-breasted top, which could be buttoned up tightly, and with a collar and satin lapels turned back to show the high "wing" collar and large, loose silk tie (cravat) which were part of the costume. The coat came to the knees and was split in the back, where a handkerchief pocket was inserted between the goods and the lining. It was usually made of heavy, smooth, black broadcloth. It was a dress coat and was worn with broadcloth or striped trousers and a "stovepipe" hat.

Privy: A small shed, often set at the back edge of a yard or lot. It had a bench with one or more oval holes and was built over a trench, and served as a toilet.

Sleepers: A child's one-piece garment, usually of Canton flannel, made with feet and a "drop seat," which could be unbuttoned, in back.

Sliding doors: Unlike the modern doors that slide over each other, the 1890 sliding double doors were pushed back into a slot between the two walls so that the doors disappeared from view. One door slid to the right and one to the left. They were pulled together to close the doorway by means of a ring sunk in the front edge of each door.

Stovepipe hat: A very high-crowned hat with a rather narrow brim. As a dress hat it was usually made of black silk.

Union suit: A close-fitting garment, combining drawers and shirt in one piece, and worn by men and children.

Wick: A lamp wick was a loosely woven tape or tube of soft spun cotton threads that drew up a steady supply of oil from the kerosene oil beneath it.

About the Author

Georgie's Capital was written to answer the questions of the author's grandchildren about how she lived "in the olden days," and is based on Mrs. Coon's own personal memories of her girlhood in Pierre, South Dakota, the locale of this story.

She holds a B.A. from Sioux Falls College and an M.A. from the University of South Dakota. In 1961, she was the recipient of a degree of Litt.D. from Sioux Falls College.

Over a period of years Mrs. Coon taught English and Classical Languages, later devoting much of her time to writing. She has had a number of poems and short stories published, but *Georgie's Capital* is her first full-length book.

About the Illustrator

CORINNE KEYSER, who has captured the engaging characteristics of nine-year old Georgie and has depicted so faithfully the charm of the Victorian era in which this story takes place, was born in New York City.

A graduate of the High School of Music and Art, she received her B.F.A. from the Tyler School of Fine Arts, of Temple University in Philadelphia. Later, she studied children's book illustration at New York University. She is married, and is the mother of two young daughters.